THE SUICIDE RUN

William Styron (1925-2006), a native of the
Tidewater region of Virginia, was a graduate of
Duke University and a veteran of the Marine
Corps. His books include *Lie Down in Darkness*,
The Long March, *Set This House on Fire*, *The
Confessions of Nat Turner*, *Sophie's Choice*, *This
Quiet Dust*, *Darkness Visible* and *A Tidewater
Morning*. He was awarded the Pulitzer Prize for
fiction, the Howells Medal, the American Book
Award and the Légion d'Honneur. With his wife,
the poet and activist Rose Styron, he lived for
most of his adult life in Roxbury, Connecticut,
and in Vineyard Haven, Massachusetts.

ALSO BY WILLIAM STYRON

WILLIAM STYRON

The Suicide Run

Five Tales of the Marine Corps

VINTAGE BOOKS
London

Published by Vintage 2011

2 4 6 8 10 9 7 5 3 1

Four of the five stories in this work have been previously published:
"Blankenship" originally appeared in *Papers on Language and
Literature*, Autumn 1987; "Marriott, the Marine" originally
appeared in *Esquire*, September 1971; "The Suicide Run" originally
appeared in the *American Poetry Review*, May/June 1974; and the
middle portion of "My Father's House" originally appeared
in *The New Yorker*, July 20, 2009

First published in Great Britain in 2010 by
Jonathan Cape

Vintage
Random House, 20 Vauxhall Bridge Road,
London SW1V 2SA

www.vintage-books.co.uk

Addresses for companies within The Random House Group Limited
can be found at: www.randomhouse.co.uk/offices.htm

The Random House Group Limited Reg. No. 954009

A CIP catalogue record for this book
is available from the British Library

ISBN 9780099532224

The Random House Group Limited supports The Forest
Stewardship Council (FSC), the leading international forest
certification organisation. All our titles that are printed on
Greenpeace approved FSC certified paper carry the FSC logo.
Our paper procurement policy can be found at:
www.rbooks.co.uk/environment

Mixed Sources
Product group from well-managed
forests and other controlled sources
www.fsc.org   Cert no. TT-COC-2139
© 1996 Forest Stewardship Council

FSC

Printed and bound in Great Britain by
CPI Bookmarque, Croydon, CR0 4TD

CONTENTS

The Suicide Run

BLANKENSHIP

A MID THE SMELLY STRETCH of riptides and treacherous currents formed by the confluence of the upper East River and Long Island Sound stands a small low-lying island. Surmounted for most of its length by ancient prison buildings, it is an island hardly distinguishable, in its time-exhausted drabness, from those dozen or so other islands occupied by prisons and hospitals which give to the New York waterways such a bleak look of municipal necessity and—for some reason especially at twilight—that air of melancholy and erosion of the spirit. Yet something here compels a second glance. Something makes this island seem even excessively ugly, and a meaner and shabbier eyesore. Perhaps this is because of the island's situation; for a prison island it just seems to be in too nice a place. It commands a fine wide view of the blue Sound to the east and the white houses on the mainland nearby—houses which, though situated in the Bronx, are so neat and scrubbed and summery-looking as to make New York City seem as remote as Nantucket. One passing by the island might more logically envision a pretty park here, or groves of trees, or a harbor for sailboats, than this squalid acre of prison buildings. Yet perhaps it's the buildings themselves which make the place look more than ordinarily grim and depressing—so that the cleanly utilitarian, white marble structures on the other of the city's islands seem, by comparison, almost beguiling sanctuaries. These date back nearly a century, soot-encrusted brick piles of turrets and fake moats and parapets and Victorian towers. With these, and with their crenellated battlements and lofty embrasures and all the sham artifices of fortressed power, the buildings possess a calculated, ridiculous ugliness, as if for someone locked within the walls they must add to the injury of simple confinement the diurnal insulting reminder—in every nook and cranny unavoidable and symbolic—of his incarceration.

Time has imparted little dignity to the place. Rain and soot and wind have weathered it, but the stain which they have printed upon those grandiose walls seems to have left no patina of mellowness, and has only made them more dirty. It would be a sad place to be. In any case, whichever makes the island so oppressive—the prospect, so close, of the clean white houses, or the prison's appalling architecture—either, to anyone held captive there, would make the idea of freedom more precious. Precious enough, indeed, that a man might risk—given enough anguish, and enough fury—the mile of channel, and the extraordinary tides.

It so happened that during most of the last war the island and prison were in the possession of the United States Navy, which had leased the place from the city in order to lock up members of its personnel—sailors and marines and coast guardsmen—who had offended against the rules and regulations. These prisoners (although the population naturally fluctuated, it rarely went below two thousand men) were not major offenders. That is to say, they were not men who had murdered or committed treason or viciously assaulted an officer or committed any crime so dreadful that the total weight of naval wrath and justice had sunk mountainously about them and had swallowed them up for twenty years. But if these men had not been guilty of supreme crimes, they were not precisely minor offenders, either: they had thieved and raped and deserted and had been caught committing buggery and had been drunk or asleep, or both, while on duty and had been, almost to a man at one time or another, away without leave. They had all received courts-martial of some sort, and their average term of sentence was three and a half years. Yet, possessing neither the respectability of innocence nor the glamour of ruthless criminals, they shared a desperate, tribal feeling of inadequacy and were often victims, even within themselves, of sour contempt. No one displayed this contempt, however, with such cocky amusement as the marines who were on the island to guard them, and who called them simply "yardbirds."

The prisoners were a sad lot, and the marines (there were two hundred of them, officers and men) ruled the island with a piratical swagger and a fine grip on the principles of intimidation. Few prisoners were ever beaten, for this in itself was a court-martial offense; but the history of bondage has shown that to slap a man about invites rebellion, while a tyranny of simple scorn cows the will and ulcerates the soul. Armed only with short billy clubs of hickory, the marines sauntered safe and serene and with a wisecracking arrogance among the fidgety horde, poking ribs and facetiously whacking behinds. The prisoners were gray with the grayness of men who seldom are exposed to light and suffer the sick, constant ache of loneliness. It was the peculiar grayness somehow stamped only upon the perpetually browbeaten—a lackluster and forlorn complexion, the hue of smoke. By day the prisoners worked—making rope in the rope shop, shoveling coal in the power plant, hauling garbage, sweeping and swabbing their barracks floors. Then there was an enormous siren, mounted atop a water tower. It was this machine, like an intransigent apocalyptic voice, which seemed to dominate the island and the proceedings of each day. Like an archangel's horn, too, it was apt to blow at any hour. It had the impact of a smack across the mouth, and at its shocking, pitiless wail the prisoners fled galloping across the island like panicked sheep, egged on by the marines' rowdy cries. Shortly then, in front of their barracks (because always perhaps *this* morning one of them, in grief and desperation, had climbed down off the seawall), they were checked and counted one by one, standing in desolate ranks beneath the wide unbounded sky and the outrageous brick battlements and towers.

But if it was the enlisted marines who so mortified the prisoners, it was the officers on the island (there were twenty-five of them, seven marine officers in charge of the guard and the rest naval men: legal experts and administrative officers, doctors and dentists, chaplains to attend to the prisoners' unmanned spirits, and a psychiatrist or two to adjust their often chaotic heads) who enjoyed sovereign and unchallengeable power, and to whom the prisoners accorded a cowering respect. At their approach the prisoners scrambled erect, removed their caps (being forbidden to salute), and stood in alarmed and rigid silence. Such were the rules, and thus even the meanest lieutenant might feel that same spinal thrill and hot flush of privilege that a cardinal must feel, or a general at parade, and sense chill little ecstasies of dominion. Yet of all these officers—including the marine colonel in charge of the island, and the ranks of brass beneath him—none was treated by the prisoners with such craven and flustered diffidence as a certain marine warrant officer named Charles R. Blankenship. This in a way was remarkable, for he was not a cruel or angry man.

Blankenship was in charge of the blockhouse, where the more violent and wicked prisoners were kept behind foot-thick doors and in ugly little cells. He was not a large man—indeed, he was of only average height—but there was a quality he had (perhaps the erect military carriage or the suppleness of his well-knit body, which was outlined always so cleanly because of the tailored cut of his uniform) that gave the impression of cool coordinated strength. Nor did he display this strength with any of the swagger or parade which sets off the toy soldier from the sober professional. His bearing, rather, was that of a man who has long ago outgrown any callow tendency to strut (had he ever possessed any at all) and wears pride in his uniform with an offhand confidence and conviction, like the suave self-assurance with which often some very beautiful woman, so long accustomed to stares and admiration, wears her beauty.

At this time Blankenship was a little over thirty years old. In the Marine Corps this is young for a warrant officer, who is usually a grizzled, fat old man who has struggled upward through the ranks to find himself, in his declining years, a kind of serene and crusty androgyne—no longer a member of the common mob yet not really an officer—who putters about in his flower beds or, slouched in potbellied salute at some twilight parade, is referred to with misty affection as "the old Gunner," and in general receives the legendary and universal respect shown to wise old codgers. It was this fact more than anything—that even in a time of war (it was then 1944), when promotions were many, he could attain at thirty what for most marines took nearly a lifetime—that reinforced Blankenship's pride in his rank and his achievement, and lent to his manner such solid assurance. It was not a swollen or presumptuous pride. It was simply the pride of one who is aware of his abilities and who feels respectably fulfilled upon having those abilities recognized, no matter how luckily expedited by the accident of war. Blankenship asked for little else. For, like many regular marines, he had never had any particular desire to become a commissioned officer—a captain or a colonel. For him it was enough to remain a *good* marine, no matter what the rank. He knew, too, that forced to revert, as would assuredly happen when the war ended, to his old rank, he would become a sergeant again—a *good* marine—without shirk or complaint or demur.

Now it developed that at dawn of a gray, blustery morning in November—almost five months to the day after his arrival on the island (and following two years of combat duty in the Pacific)—an event occurred which for the first time disrupted the orderly pattern of Blankenship's daily routine. An escape, or what appeared to be one—the first in nearly a year—had been discovered by one of the guards as he made his regular rounds through the chill and misty light. As he told it later (he was a burly young marine from Kentucky with an adolescent voice which cracked excitedly, and the highly informed, solemn air of one who knows he is a participant, maybe even the key figure, in something momentous), the asphalt parapets along the seawall were shrouded in fog, so thick in fact that he had had to walk, as he put it, "right cautious" in order to keep from falling into the sea and even his dog, a great vicious Doberman with milk-white tusks which could crush through a man's wrist or calf bone like so much soft clay, had lost his footing once and had stopped to sniff the murk and raise his head to whimper. Had it not been for the wind, the escape might have gone unnoticed until the morning count, much later. As it was, the marine said, it was the wind that had tipped him off, that bore to his ears through the impenetrable, somber dawn a faint *flap-flap-flapping*, a steady sound like that of a loose tin signboard, or of metal banging against brick. Which in fact it was, just that: a heavy window section forced open, bars, rivets, and all, from the washroom of a barracks not twenty feet away, and left dangling against the wall. It was a deft clean job, done with a crowbar or a pipe; yet how, everyone speculated later, it had been accomplished without arousing the slumbering prison was more than a mystery, for it should have made a noise like the shrieks of the damned—prying loose from reinforced concrete nearly a quarter ton of steel. At any rate, the marine called the corporal of the guard, and the corporal hustled up to the officers' wardroom and woke Blankenship, who happened to be officer of the day.

"So it was just your misfortune to have the duty, wasn't it, Gunner?" said Colonel Wilhoite, with a wide smile, later on in the morning.

"Yes sir," Blankenship said, "it's tough. But somebody's

got to have the duty. Five of us stand it, plus those seven officers. We all figure we've got one chance in twelve for an escape to land on our day. My number just came up wrong, that's all. Tough."

"Sit down, Gunner. Have a cigarette." This was the colonel's office, one of those arid military chambers, bare save for desk and chairs, a single filing cabinet, and two framed photographs of the commandant and a youthful, sprightlier Franklin D. Roosevelt. Past the windows was the Sound, blue and glossy now with oblong shapes of sunlight. A tugboat hooted lugubriously in its passage seaward. The colonel sighed.

"Remarkable, simply remarkable," he whispered. "A boat. You say they built a boat."

Blankenship lowered himself into a chair and lit a cigarette. "They certainly did, sir. There was this shed near the carpenter's shop. It was what you call a hobby project. There were just these two guys. The chief who runs the place thought they were building birdhouses or something. Anyway, they were making birdhouses whenever he looked in. Then we found it broken into this morning—the shed, that is. They had sawhorses rigged up. They even had made templates for the thing. Then we saw this track across the ground to the seawall, just the sort of a track a seven- or eight-foot skiff would make being dragged across the ground."

"Remarkable," said the colonel again, "simply ingenious. Imagine, building a boat. How perfectly remarkable."

"Our boats were out since six, also the harbor police. They found no trace, so they must be ashore."

"Ransacking some house in Great Neck, no doubt." The

colonel paused, inspecting the tips of his fingers, then looked up to contemplate, with dreamy, moist eyes, the far reaches of the Sound. "I must say it was most remarkable." Wilhoite was a round man of about fifty with thinning gray hair and a florid elastic face upon which an exceedingly stunted and inconsequential nose had been implanted, like a pittance or an afterthought. It was a feature which detracted from a face that otherwise might have been formidable and strong, and may have been a factor which had helped to prevent him from becoming a general. He had distinguished himself in action at Belleau Wood, but a touch of asthma and other things had kept him from seeing combat in this war.

Blankenship, waiting, watched him narrowly. So far, Wilhoite had proved unpredictable, and Blankenship had not been very successful in his attempts to gauge what was forthcoming from the man. He would not yet be so extreme as to call the colonel a fool, but there was something about him which was silly and erratic, that much was true. He was a man of changey moods, a generally amiable person who ran his affairs with a sort of harried competence. He had freely admitted to Blankenship his ignorance of prisoners, asking plaintively why, of all places, headquarters should have sent him here. This candor, Blankenship felt, had in a human sort of way been to his credit. But it embarrassed Blankenship—with a crawling, inward discomfort—to know that he knew more than his commanding officer, and that Wilhoite—with his awkwardly solicitous, ingratiating over-familiarity—*knew* he knew more, too. With sudden ugly pain at this thought, and with the confusion of the last few hours still boiling about in his mind, Blankenship, who had

been peering up at Wilhoite as he gazed dreamily, chin on
fingertips, out to sea, turned uneasily away, thinking that he
had known superior officers who had been bullies and
drunkards and cowards, or all three, but never before one to
whom his own attitude stopped, for some reason, just so
short of actual indifference.

The colonel finally spoke. "Look, Gunner, we can't pin
this on anyone. We're just lucky we've had such a good
record so far." He paused, sucking his lips. "Look, you had
brig duty in the Old Corps. How the hell do you think we
can stop this sort of thing? If those birds did it so easily,
there are two thousand others around here who'll get the
same idea."

Even as he spoke Blankenship had almost parted with
the words, having stored them up a half hour before, having
sensed, somehow, that he would be asked. Yet now he chose
his manner of speaking, avoiding brusqueness and, above
all, condescension: "One, sir, I'd double the guard on foggy
nights. Two, I'd suggest securing and lock-bolting all those
old window frames. Then I'd shake down—right now—every
barracks and cell block on the island and get rid of any old
stored-up pipes and crowbars. As for boats, sir, that's a bit
outside my experience, but I'd certainly keep a tight watch
on my tools and lumber."

The words were out, the advice delivered. Blankenship
felt a vague sense of shame, almost as if, a child, he had
been beset by his own father for some scrap of wisdom. He
wished the interview were over.

"And they were—who, Gunner?" Pencil poised, the
colonel waited while Blankenship said all he knew, giving
him the same dry and tedious details—the names of the two

men, their home addresses, convictions and sentences and conduct in confinement—that he had hastily that morning memorized from the record books and had already told the colonel not five minutes before. He had prepared himself for this, too, with casual almost unthinking efficiency born out of ten years' habit which forced him to consider in times of crisis not only the crisis itself but its future complications. It was one of the talents he had which had gotten him his warrant, and he knew it—a reflex as effortless as breathing which caused him to grasp an emergency at its core while aware each second of its all but invisible growths and tendrils, too, its imminent threats and its chances for exploitation. It was a talent which applied in this situation—an exasperating flight of two yardbirds who should never have been allowed to be in a position to escape at all—with no more or less fitness than it had applied on Guadalcanal, where with a mortar-blasted hunk of flesh as big as a small fist gouged out of his leg, flat on the ground with the hot funky stench of jungle in his nose, he had kept up for a night and a day a telephoned hourly situation report to Division, "thus contributing substantially to interunit liaison and to the success of the operation," his Silver Star citation had read, and thus being, as General Stokes had afterward told him himself, "the only goddam operations chief in the goddam division who ever remembered to let us know what the hell was going on."

Blankenship felt the wound now, as he had ten times a day in whatever damp weather and probably would for the rest of his life, an icy trembling twitch like electric voltage pulsating in his thigh: for a brief dolorous instant it battened cruel teeth down to the marrow of his bone; then the trembling ceased. He shifted his leg, with the pain vexing him all the more because he had had to repeat these things to the colonel, and as he finished his report and the colonel began fussily to rummage through a drawer, Blankenship felt his irritation grow and grow, along with a frustrated and powerless outrage at this morning's mess, which could have been so easily prevented but which, more importantly, had left him feeling so cheated and unfulfilled. Nor was it an anger directed so much against the colonel now, or the two escaped prisoners (whom he had never laid eyes on except for their record-book pictures), but against some totally abstract concept of order, an order which—for the moment at least— had allowed itself to become corrupted and in default. For when the corporal of the guard had aroused him hours before, breathing into his ear the word "escape," the word had shocked him from slumber like ice water and, even as he methodically but without one second's hesitation drew on his clothes, heavy scarf and gloves and field jacket, had made him feel a slow mounting thrill of anticipation so intense and freighted with promise that it was like a sort of ecstasy.

He had felt it before, this cold excitement involving something to which he could hardly assign a name— challenge, perhaps, or summons to duty—at any rate a quickening of his senses so clamorous and memorable that in long periods when it was not there he had found himself waiting for it, waiting for the crisis with the tranquil, fierce patience of a communicant awaiting the moment of passion, or a hunter in the marsh watching the final defenseless swoop of birds. It was as if this morning he had once again and for the first time since Guadalcanal been given the call, ordained to bring to some sudden threat of disequilibrium a calm and unshakable sense of order. And he had rushed out into the swirling white dawn with a chill of delight up his back and with his mind clicking like an adding machine. Yet now as he watched the colonel rifling clumsily through his papers, something close to despair returned as he recalled how, instead of the escape being nipped off neatly, the sheep back in their fold, his very first glance at the ruptured window and bars separated so beautifully from their pinnings had told him that, this time, he would have little chance for triumph.

"I can't find the main number of the F.B.I.," the colonel said.

"I already called them, sir," Blankenship put in.

The colonel looked up. "I should have known," he said mildly. "I forgot. It's in your special orders, isn't it? And—"

"I called the rest, sir. The harbor and city police and the state police. I finally woke up some dogface over at Fort Slocum, and then I called the police in New Rochelle and in Nassau County. I also put in calls to the cops in those birds' hometowns—Decatur, Illinois, and some little place in Wisconsin. They said they'd have their eyes peeled."

A look of bafflement came over the colonel's face, and perhaps of hurt, too, as if he had become impaled upon the keen cutting edge of Blankenship's finesse. "By God, Gunner," he said with a cramped little grin, "you got these birds all taped up." He rose stiffly and went to the window and stood swaying there, dumpy and morose, hands locked behind him. There was little else to do, the two men were irretrievably gone, and Blankenship wished to be dismissed. He had not taped up anything; he had seized every proliferating growth of the emergency save its essential core. He had not caught those men—that was that—and he felt stuffed with sodden, inert disappointment, remembering how not four hours before and in spite of the sight of the neatly professional breakout he had still been possessed by that familiar chill, immaculate excitement, and his mind had worked with a clarity so pure, so aerial and flawless, that it seemed as if mounds of cobwebs had been torn away from his vision, and that he was suddenly looking for the first time at everything around him through the sheerest transparent glass. And how at that moment something more than logic—an intuition, rather—had told him that those yardbirds had built a boat. Even now he could only guess at how he had arrived at that remarkable judgment, a judgment which turned out to be not only remarkable but true; he only knew that he had known it, and instantly, with as much certitude as he knew his own name, rank, and serial number, and that armed with this certitude he had been spared going through the seven or eight hapless, groping steps of another man.

He had ordered the alarm sounded, and an immediate count, sending two squads of the guard up to the work area to hunt for a place or shed where a boat might have been built or hidden. And so not ten minutes later, tearing back from the armory through the greenly mounting light, strapping on his pistol, he was neither surprised nor even particularly gratified to hear some sergeant call out through the mist and over the shrill fantastic racket of the siren: "Gunner, we found a shed . . . a boat was—" because he already knew. He hadn't answered, but had just galloped to the dock and commandeered one of the patrol boats he had ordered warmed up five minutes before, despairing even then—as the light came up dimly and revealed a Sound motionless and bare of all except a flock of swooping gulls—of finding anything, but touched still, almost to his soul, with this strange combination of fury and joy.

The colonel turned. "Gunner, just how did you know they had built this goddam boat, or skiff? Macklin told me you were out there on the water snooping around for a boat less than ten minutes after the alarm went off. If the guard had found that sprung window an hour before you'd probably have gotten those birds."

"Well, one, sir, I figured they knew they'd freeze to death if they hit the water in this kind of weather. Two, the ferry stops at midnight. If they were going to try and smuggle themselves out in a truck or something on the ferry, they certainly wouldn't make a breakout at night but just hide themselves sometime during the day and then try to get aboard. Three, the foggy night. Perfect to get lost in . . ." Blankenship halted. "I don't know, sir. I guess I just *felt* this thing."

"Remarkable, remarkable," Wilhoite muttered and fell silent. He returned to his desk and sat down. Then he smiled, his words broadly explanatory, apologetic, and rather relieved, as if he had abruptly shifted from his shoulders a pack full of sand: "Well look, Gunner, it's nobody's fault, as I said. We've had a good record. I don't think the Bureau will be down our necks for this. I'll just put those recommendations of yours in effect and—" He raised his eyebrows and paused, and there was the same puzzling smile on his harried, honest face; but if his expression was meant to indicate some unspoken, possibly mysterious understanding between them, Blankenship had no idea what it was. For a moment the look seemed to transmit a sort of shy, quiet admiration, but whatever it might be Blankenship felt embarrassed and looked away.

"Yes sir?"

The smile faded. "Nothing, Gunner," he said briskly. "I think that'll be all." When he arose, Blankenship got up, too. But then the voice became soft again, even wistful. "God, how I hate this job. I envy you First Division boys. Why the hell I couldn't have gotten one of those Saipan regiments, instead of this . . . hooligans and eight-balls and jerks. I've put in sixteen letters in the past year but every goddam time I hear BuMed has turned me down on account of my lousy wheezing chest . . ." As he spoke Blankenship wished to shut his ears against this labored, querulous confession, but even so felt a mild tug of sympathy for such a man, past hope of glory and with time running out, who could still entertain some lustrous vision of fulfillment. Separated by a star and a pay grade and slight asthma from the goal of his life, he had already begun to wither. Old soldiers never died, it was true, especially if they were generals, but old colonels did; for among such reasons as that, Blankenship was content with his own world, where a man out of the pure comprehension of his duty might sometimes feel the keen, rapturous excitement he had felt that morning, and need not finally end up with skull battered to a pulp against a wall of politics and chance and ambition, like Wilhoite, in whose eyes already were specters of battles unseen and medals unwon and the slow final ooze of unlaureled retirement—of lawn chairs and rose gardens and horseshoes pitched in slumberous, dying arcs against the palms of St. Petersburg. The thought depressed Blankenship; he wished the colonel would stop talking and let him go. But when he finally did cease, with the words "That's how it is, Gunner, those bastards at headquarters have you over a barrel every time," Blankenship forced himself to smile—out of some momentary, curious sympathy.

"I know what you mean, Colonel," he said. "I don't much like brig duty, either."

There was a knock at the door, which opened without a second's pause to let in a chill gust of air from the corridors and a pretty blond woman of about thirty, sleek in furs. "Darling," she said breathlessly, "I have to have— Oh, *excuse* me, I didn't know anyone—"

"Suzie, I've *told* you—" the colonel began.

Blankenship moved toward the door. "That's all right, Mrs. Wilhoite, I was just going."

"Suzie, I've told you—"

"Webby, I *have* to get the eleven o'clock ferry, and I've *got* to have some money if I'm to see the caterers and do all those things—"

"Excuse me, Mrs. Wilhoite," Blankenship murmured, squeezing by.

"I'm sorry, darling," she went on, "but I do have— Oh, Mr. Blankenship, you *are* coming to the party, aren't you?"

"Which party is that, Mrs. Wilhoite?"

"Which *one*? The Thanks*giving* party, of course, tomorrow night. You are Mr. Blankenship, aren't you?"

"Yes," he said, then quickly: "I mean yes, I'm coming, and I am Mr. Blankenship."

She gave a small bright laugh, which he found himself echoing, rather foolishly, with a faint grin. "Oh good," she said. "So many of you officers we never see, and I always get you confused with that—what's his name?—Lieutenant—"

"Darling," the colonel put in, "if you're going to make that ferry—"

She turned and Blankenship slid away, pulling on his gloves. Outside the building, a cold damp blast of air struck him; he shivered, slanting his eyes toward the sky. It had become suddenly dim. Eclipse-like, a luminous corona surrounded the sun, and a shifting rack of mist, outriders of those great gray clouds which all morning had mounted to the north, brought a stiff wind and the promise of snow. The asphalt expanse of ground was deserted, except for a dozen gray prisoners in the distance, marching dejectedly in column and guarded by a lone marine. Against the advancing overcast the buildings, the brick towers and battlements, seemed to take on a sudden baronial and oppressive splendor; here and there lights winked on, though it was nearly noon. There was something in the scene hinting too much at the final white onset of winter; to Blankenship, with the climate of the tropics still steaming in his blood, it was touched by a vague sense of menace. Quickly descending the steps, he hurried toward his blockhouse, passing clumps of prisoners, pinched with cold, who arranged themselves in frozen and panicky attention when he approached. Yet as he muttered the usual "As you were," he gave the prisoners hardly a glance, beset as he was with the same troubled feeling of anger and impotence he had had in the colonel's office, which he had thought a breath of cold air might cure, but hadn't.

Nor was it only the escape now, although as he thought of the escape again another pang of failure came like the quick blow of a fist at the pit of his stomach, when he remembered how in the boat at dawn, rounding a point of rocks—pistol unlimbered and feet braced against the spray-drenched gunwales and with the siren roaring in his ears like the ascending demented howls of souls chained in hell— he had thought, in one final and illusory moment of self-deception, that he had spotted those bastards. He had not, of course. What had appeared to be, in that fraudulent and compromising light, a boat had turned out to be nothing but a cardboard box heaved over some ship's side. It had not been the quarry which he felt at that instant he would have literally sacrificed a leg or an arm to capture, but a maddening piece of driftage upon which the words HORMEL FINE SOUPS had been written and which, with its mirage-like deceit, gave him a second's furious resolve to strangle the manufacturer of both soup and box. For he felt he had been tricked in the race at every turn. It was as if those yardbirds had been handicapped two lengths instead of the one length that was fair and just, and to this excessive advantage had been added the ultimate merciless ridicule of cunningly strewn debris, like soup boxes, in the wake of their victory. He had been tricked, all right, and as he strode toward the blockhouse entry he felt suddenly so abortively hollow and outmaneuvered that the feeling was close to exhaustion. Something else troubled him, too—something he knew he *should* be worrying about—but this, whatever it was, he banished from his mind when, at the entry to the blockhouse, he saw the look on Sergeant Mulcahy's face and knew that more trouble was in the air.

Mulcahy's chronically jaundiced expression was only in part due to the sourness of his nature, for he was still recovering from malaria. He was gaunt, ugly, with a crooked nose—a regular with fifteen years' service. His contempt for the prisoners was both artless and profound. It was based simply, as he had expressed it to Blankenship, on the fact that the convicts, whom he referred to categorically as "skunks," had all been experiencing blissful sexual connections in New York or Chicago while he was "out contracting the jungle rot." He might have been a bully, except that his spleen had become so enfeebled by malaria and general world- and war-weariness that his only cruelty was an occasional drowsy prod or poke. "A little goosin' don't hurt 'em none," he had said to Blankenship, but it was something which now and then he had to be called down on. At this moment his dilapidated, sulfurous face wore a look of the plainest disgust.

"What's up?" Blankenship said.

"Ah, there's some guy here thinks he's top dog."

"New man?" The gate swung open slowly, eased to behind Blankenship with a pneumatic hiss.

"Did you get those two birds this morning, Gunner?"

Mulcahy's irrelevance, together with the renewed reminder of his failure, so annoyed him that he turned and snapped: "I *said*, goddammit, Mulcahy, is he a new man?"

Mulcahy drooped. "Yes, sir. Five days piss and punk."

"For what?"

"Fighting. He just come in from B Company. Colonel had him up for office hours this morning."

Blankenship entered the office, a corner room with enormous barred windows, while Mulcahy shambled in behind. "So what's the trouble, then?" he said, sitting down. "What cell's he assigned to?"

"Fifteen, sir. Well, Gunner, he just wouldn't cooperate. This skunk comes in here with a bunch of smart-guy crap, saying how much he didn't like the smell in here and all and how it 'irritated' him—that's the word he used, Gunner, I swear to God—to have an outside cell where there was no view and only blower ventilation, and all. He was just running off at the mouth, that's all. I mean I never saw such a smart son of a bitch—"

"So—" Blankenship, staring Mulcahy down, felt the blood rushing to his eyes in anger, and saw the sergeant's freckled, sallow face sheepishly begin to crumble. "So—" he repeated.

"Well, Gunner, it was just a little tap right over the eye—"

"God*dammit*, Mulcahy!" His fist thumped hard, painfully, on the desk, in a fury made thrice potent by the events of the morning. "I told you to keep your goddam Irish paws off these prisoners—"

"Gunner, I swear before God—" Protectively, Mulcahy rolled back his bleary yellow eyes. "It didn't even make a br— draw blood," he stammered. "I put a—"

"Quiet!"

"Yes, sir."

"I've told you for the last time. You lay hands on these birds anymore and I'll have you up before the colonel in two seconds. Do you understand that?"

"Yes, sir," he said glumly.

"O.K. Now go get that man and bring him here."

"Aye-aye, sir."

"And give me that club," he added, holding out his hand. "Some of you people are so goddam Asiatic you'd beat your own grandmother."

Mulcahy exited in gangling, clumsy haste. Blankenship

sank back in his chair, calmer now, faintly ashamed at his outburst, and reflecting that, after all and in spite of everything, Mulcahy was a good marine, and likable even if he was stunningly ignorant. But as he slumped slowly back, anticipating a few seconds' rest—perhaps a catnap, even, to clear from his mind the morning's tension—the siren, howling for the midday count, went off above him. It was a sound which, being so familiar, should not have disturbed him, but now in his frustration and weariness the noise seemed to pour through the walls in wildly ascending and racking gusts and, reaching its crescendo, to probe into his eardrums like lancets. One window was cracked open; he got up, scattering papers, and slammed it down. As he turned again, he noticed that his hands were trembling—a phenomenon so rare and strange that it caused him a fleeting sense of panic. Perhaps it was only a cold coming on, perhaps a recurrence of his malaria. He walked toward the wash basin, meaning to inspect his eyes in the mirror, but at this moment there was a knock. The door opened; as it did, the siren ceased its clamor, falling swiftly earthward in a remorseful sullen groan.

"This here is the man, Gunner," said Mulcahy.

Blankenship sat down, shooed Mulcahy out, and looked up to meet the prisoner's gaze.

"What's your name?" he said.

"McFee."

For a moment Blankenship said nothing, for there was something familiar about this man; he was certain he had seen him before. This certainty was in itself curious enough, since few prisoners had memorable faces but only drab achromatic promontories upon which noses, mouths, and ears were struck like gray and similar shapes of putty. What was more striking now was the man's expression. That, too, Blankenship recalled, from wherever and whenever it was: an aspect at first glance no different, in its wan sun-sheltered anonymity, from all the rest of the prisoners, yet swiftly and hauntingly unique—intelligence, perhaps? Perhaps no more than something in his level blue eyes which seemed halfway between scorn and defiance. Then Blankenship remembered: the face floating toward him through cigarette smoke and a confusion of laughter, a voice—"Drink, sir?"—too straightforward to be insolent yet touched with a whisper of mockery, and a parting smile, finally—like the one he wore now—that was not so much a smile as a smirk, expressing some mysterious and inner satisfaction. Of course. He had seen this man months before, working as a waiter at the only one of the colonel's parties he had ever been to.

"Look, McFee," he said at length, "I don't know what kind of language you've been getting away with over at the colonel's quarters, but over here when you're asked your name you give your *full* name and you give your serial number and you say *sir*. Do you understand that? Now let's *have* it."

"McFee, Lawrence M., 180611." There was a pause, one which though somehow avoiding disrespect still flirted perilously with the notion of contempt, and the *"sir"* came only a cagey half second before the crucial, unbearable instant. It was odd, bold, and Blankenship felt a surge of anger, not so much at this behavior as at the fact that he himself suddenly felt, here among two thousand spineless and craven snobs, a sneaking admiration for such talented arrogance. He continued to gaze at McFee. It was a young face—twenty-five or twenty-six, he judged—with features usually described as "clean-cut," and unshrinking blue eyes. Without his miserable denims he might have been taken for a college football star, for he was big and broad-shouldered, and even standing now at attention he had all the relaxed, supercilious grace of a campus athlete.

"What's the matter with you, McFee? The duty sergeant told me you've been giving him a hard time."

"He tried to strong-arm me."

"Mulcahy told me you were beating your gums about the accommodations we've got over here."

"I was," he said calmly. "They stink. I said so and your fucking gorilla clobbered me."

This outspoken audacity so took him aback that Blankenship rose from where he was sitting, strolled to a spot within a foot of McFee, and propped himself on the edge of the desk. "They do, do they? They stink, huh?" As he spoke, confused and casting about for words, he was aware that he was managing to control his voice—a remarkable fact considering the fury he felt rising at this man's insolence, and which was not so much directed at the insolence itself but at the cool, even fearless self-possession with which he assumed it. Now he was so close to McFee that he could feel the warm steady breathing that crossed the short space of air between them and was aware, for the first time, of the round welt on McFee's forehead where, indeed, Mulcahy must have swatted him. The welt was an inconsequential blob of swollen pinkish flesh, but it was nonetheless a visible and now accusatory brand, a tiny ensign of oppression and illegal abuse. For the moment it gave McFee a slight but telling advantage, and it aggravated Blankenship's silent fury.

He had never had a prisoner face up to him before. Because it baffled him he stalled briefly for time, and altered his tack. "What did you want to get caught fighting for, McFee? You had a nice soft job in the colonel's house. Now you'll just be another one of the bums. You must have had a pretty good confinement record to have gotten such a nice job. What are you, a swabjockey?"

"I wish the fuck I was."

"You a hooligan?"

"I'm a marine," he said, with a trace of bitterness, and also of disdain. He stood there steadfast and massive, with his irritating animal grace and with his breath coming warmly and steadily from the set contemptuous smile on his lips. Along with his anger, Blankenship felt a chilly shiver of excitement, as if he had received a personal and even physical challenge from this defiance. And although both his conscience and regulations forbade him to, he felt now, too, an irresistible desire to bait and goad—something he'd never lower himself to do with an ordinary prisoner.

"You're *not* a marine, McFee," he said quietly, "not anymore. You're a yardbird. A bum. Didn't you know that?" He paused, while for a second, in an attempt to stare each other down, their eyes met hot and unwavering. "You're swill. Slop. You're not any more of a marine than Shirley Temple. You're lower than whale shit on the bottom of the sea. You know the saying, don't you, McFee?" Yet while he spoke he felt a mild mean twinge, as if he were degrading not McFee but himself by using all the stale worn-out obscenities employed numbingly and twenty-four hours a day by every beef-witted sergeant on the island. And staring at McFee while he said them, seeing the look of contempt widen, enlarge, lines of amusement springing into his eyes, Blankenship halted, then said, "What did you do, McFee? Desert? Like all the rest of these patriotic citizens?"

"If you look in my record book, Gunner, that's the word they use. I call it something else."

"What do you call it?"

"I call it liberate."

"Liberate from what?"

"How about letting me stand at ease?" McFee said. Instead of a request it sounded like a suggestion, and one so astonishingly bold and crusty that Blankenship heard himself say "At ease" before he had even thought about it. Relaxed, McFee absently fingered the bruise on his forehead and said, in a level cold voice: "If you believe in something you desert from it. When you don't believe in something anymore you can't desert from it. You liberate yourself. That's what I did."

His voice had an austere quality, frigid with conviction. It was a voice free of sloppy accents—not cultivated, not even educated perhaps, simply reasonable even when obscene. Without explanation, the sense of authority in the voice stirred in Blankenship a strange and fugitive sort of respect but—possibly because of this respect—sent renewed outrage pulsing through his muscles and bones. He could feel the tension in his rump and in his arms as he sat there and heard the words, saw McFee's great graceful body go loose, slumped in an attitude of slovenly, insouciant power.

"You can't rebel against the Marine Corps, McFee," he said.

"Who says you can't? So they handed me six years for it. But I goddam well rebelled."

"Your soul might still belong to God, McFee, but your ass belongs to me. And the penal code of the United States Navy."

"So what?" he sneered.

"So it means you're double-screwed. Haven't you got a conscience, McFee? Even a bum has a conscience. It means you didn't escape anything at all. What makes you think you were liberated when they sent you up for six years? You not only got six years to do but you got the knowledge every minute that some other poor bastard is out there doing the fighting and the dying that you chickened out on. Doesn't that keep you awake at night?"

For a second McFee swayed on his heels, lounging carelessly, saying nothing. But the smirk was still there; the irises of his eyes were like thin blue flakes of splintered glass, twinkly with scorn. Then he said, "Semper Fidelis. You people make me laugh. In peacetime you regulars couldn't get a job swabbing up piss in a poolroom."

Blankenship could not remember when he struck. It was certainly not at this moment, for later that evening as he sat in the deserted wardroom he recalled that some other words had passed between them. Of that much he was at least sure, even as he listened vacantly to dance music from the radio and raised his eyes from time to time to watch snowfall sifting a hushed blizzard across the darkened Sound, his mind bewitched by all the whiskey he had drunk—a pint—and fumbling hopefully still for some excuse to mitigate his crushing sense of guilt. There had been the escape itself, it was true, which had made him testy, unhinged him—but

Christ, he'd been unhinged before in *battles;* was this enough to justify such a flagrant sin against the law—the first one he could remember having committed in ten years' service? As for McFee—well, what about McFee? The knowledge which Blankenship had now (the record book on the radio console before him and the court-martial transcript with its ninety pages of closely typed flimsy) could not nullify the insult and arrogance which had pushed him into the act, nor could he have been expected to know these things then. Yet the facts were unavoidably there (a letter of commendation for "meritorious conduct" on New Georgia, two Purple Hearts) and the circumstances of the court-martial (six years for desertion, but a brutally long six years not because his admirable record had been ignored, which it hadn't, but because according to the testimony of the M.P.s who had finally tracked him down from San Diego all the way to Tampa, Florida, he had resisted arrest so passionately and with such homicidal fury—backed up in a restaurant where from behind the counter he had fired six shots from a Smith & Wesson .22 revolver at the arresting officers, nicking the ear of the F.B.I. man who had tagged along for the show, and resorting finally to cups, ketchup bottles, and, in a final spasm, even his own wristwatch as "missiles")—the facts were there, and as Blankenship sat cracking his knuckles in the chilly wardroom, they added to his guilt a vague sense of shame. It was not that, even now, he felt any sympathy for McFee: he had sinned and was being justly punished. He only felt that, having broken regulations by an act so violent that it put himself, at any rate theoretically, in position for a court-martial, it should have been a lesser, meaner man than McFee who had impelled him to do it. And the least he himself could have done was use his fists.

Then he remembered when he struck. It was no more than a minute later when, with the blood pulsing like hot broth through his temples, he heard McFee say finally, "Gunner, why don't you people wise up? The whole Marine Corps is one big jail. *You're* the yardbird, Gunner," repeating through the thin infuriating smirk, "You're the yardbird, Gunner," that his hand went tight and moist with sweat around Mulcahy's club on the desk behind him, and he felt the muscles of his shoulders clumping up in a knot of pain as, almost unthinking, he brought the stick down in one heavy crunching blow against McFee's cheek; even as it struck he saw McFee's mountainous frame swing back in punch-drunk and deadened collision with the wall, eyes marveling at his own impact but abulge and white with a sort of absolute certitude and defiance, still mouthing as he sagged downward: "You're the yardbird, you son of a bitch."

MARRIOTT,
THE MARINE

I

In the spring of 1951, when I was called back as a marine reserve to serve in the Korean War, I was in my mellow midtwenties though I felt like a beaten man. A number of years ago I wrote a fictional narrative based loosely on this period in my life, and it is possible that those who may have read that work will, in the account that follows, discern a few familiar echoes, since I am certain to trespass here and there upon that earlier, restless mood. Basically, I am an unaggressive, even pacific type, civilian to the marrow, and the very idea of military life sets up a doleful music in my brain—no fifes, no pipes, no gallant trumpet calls, only a slow gray dirge of muffled drums. In my reveries of the Marine Corps it is for some reason almost always raining. Engulfed in a sweltering poncho, I am standing in a downpour; with absolute clarity I can recall how, once waiting in a chow line during an Hawaiian cloudburst, I watched transfixed as my mess kit slowly filled to the brim with greasy water. Or my thoughts wander and I ponder the old monotony, the waiting—the truly vicious, intolerable waiting—then the indecent hustle, the offensive food, the sweat and the flies, the lousy pay, the anxiety and fear, the fruitless jabber, the racket of rifle fire, the degrading celibacy, the trivial, evanescent friendships, the whole humiliating baggage of a caste system calculated to bring out in men their basest vanities. I am capable of brooding on such matters with self-punishing persistence, with mixed anguish and pleasure, as one relives so often some ugly ordeal successfully endured.

No, the Marine Corps is no place for a man of my sluggish, contemplative stripe. Yet any such prolonged experience is likely to generate its own unique nostalgia, if that's the proper word (many ex-convicts, I've learned, confess to dreaming ambivalent dreams about their past incarceration), and besides, the Marine Corps is not the army or the navy but something intransigently itself. Maybe I should own up to an awful, private truth and this is that, despite the foregoing strictures, the Marine Corps has left me with a residual respect—certainly fascination—which, demeaning as it may be, I find it impossible to uproot after all these years. The result is that compulsively, like a voyeur who fights his urge yet is from time to time drawn to public bathhouses, I am led back to those lucidly recollected scenes, forced despite myself to try to make that fearsome institution give up one or two of its innermost secrets.

Anyway, the second call to duty nearly wiped me out. I had served three years in the marines during the Second World War. I had been a fire-eater then, a real trooper, and possessed the loutish devotion to duty that belonged to the extremely young of my generation. A volunteer, I had worked my way up from buck private to second lieutenant, spending most of my time at camps in the United States but receiving enough of a dose of misery in the Pacific near the war's end to discourage me from pursuing the military service as a livelihood. I was discharged and set free to finish my college education and subsequently to make my earnest, fledgling way in the world of letters. A year or so later, through a subterfuge which played upon both my inertia and my ego, and which I was dumb enough to fall for, the Marine Corps enticed me back into its purview. Offered a promotion in rank, to *first* lieutenant, and a reserve status which required no duty or drill, no responsibility, no commitment other than that I be available in the event of a future emergency (and how remote such a danger seemed back there within the minatory shadow of the atomic bomb), I took the bait with what must be regarded as amazing innocence, truly a victim of the age of the soft sell. When orders (in quintuplicate) came, less than four years later, to report for duty to the Second Marine Division in North Carolina, my woe and shock became almost insupportable—partly due to the knowledge of my own complicity in the matter. But bloody wars and the might of nations, as Bismarck observed, are built upon such witless acquiescence.

Since this account is not about myself, really, but about Paul Marriott—who at the time I am describing was a lieutenant colonel in the regular marines—I do not want to use more space than is necessary in dwelling upon the circumstances that led up to our relationship. But in all honesty I cannot skimp the whole frenzied atmosphere, the mood of despondency—"despair" would not be too strong a word—which surrounded me and my friends as we enacted our

solemn rehearsal for another war. For if I had not felt so trau-
matized, so out of place, so forsaken in this new yet achingly familiar environment, had I not been half-consciously
searching for someone with whom I might come to a reasonably civilized understanding, Paul Marriott might have
passed unnoticed and we would not have sought each other
out, and I might have failed to discover this exceptional man
whom the Marine Corps had nurtured and honored. So if
only for my own satisfaction I must try to describe my frame
of mind at the time, and recount some of the details of the
predicament so many of us found ourselves trapped in that
spring and the following months.

It may be easily guessed that at this point I had under-
gone a fairly thorough transformation. Vanished were the
ideals of duty and sacrifice. I had been to college and had
cultivated the humane studies and had come to develop a
strong aversion to warfare, along with many of my contemporaries; after the thrill of an illusory and romantic "victory"
in World War II had palled, we began to be chilled by a pre-
monition that the terminal act of that drama—the defeat
and surrender of Japan—was not an ending but a prelude to
a succession of wars as senseless and as bestial as any ever
seen. Moreover, I had a particularly selfish reason to want to
remain a civilian: to be recalled to duty at this moment in my
life seemed an especially outrageous swindle. It was not only
that I had fallen comfortably into a bohemian way of life, living in Greenwich Village, where I let my hair grow long and
accustomed myself to rising as late as two in the afternoon.
I had also written a novel, which was about to be published
and which showed the unusual signs of becoming—for a
first novel—brilliantly successful. I had suffered long and

hard on this work, pouring into it all the passion and vitality that the gods squander on youth, and while I was satisfied (as much as one ever can be) with my achievement in terms of its art, I was deep down no tiresome eccentric and hankered also after the side benefits that accrue to single young men whose first novels are brilliantly successful: toast of the world, flattered, fussed over, with a thick wallet and suavely tailored flannels, dining at the Colony and Chambord and plowing my way through galaxies of movie starlets and seraglios of wenchy Park Avenue matrons perishing with need of my favors. Almost completely an illusion, to be sure, but one which I burningly entertained; the contrast between this vision and the imminent reality—freezing on some bleak Korean tundra with the stench of cordite in my nostrils, and a heart congealed with terror—seemed to comprise an irony beyond all fathoming. But there was nothing to be done. Like a sleepwalker, I prepared to return to war. I got my hair cut and retrieved from storage my green winter uniform, which (though the jacket fit a bit tight around the middle) was intact, except for the cap, half-devoured by moths, and the cordovan shoes that were mildewed past repair.

Even the day of my departure for service had a special quality of inauspiciousness which I have never forgotten. A week or so before, President Truman had prudently removed General Douglas MacArthur from his post as commander of United Nations and American forces in the Far East—an action which, it may be remembered, drove tens of millions of Americans into a spasm of bellicose rage. By chance, the afternoon I was to leave by train for the South was the same afternoon that MacArthur had chosen to make his triumphal parade through New York City. I was in my uniform again for the first time. For some reason I recall that day with abnormal clarity: the beatific light of April, pigeons wheeling against a sky incomparably blue, trees in full bud along the Upper East Side streets, vast crowds massing along Fifth Avenue, and in wordless singsong over all—with rhythmic rise and fall like the distant swarming of millions of small insects—the avid buzz of patriotic hysteria. I had never heard that sinister, many-throated voice quite so loud nor so unmistakably before; it seemed an offense to the lovely day, and at least in part to escape it I ducked into the dark bar of the Sherry-Netherland, where with the girl who was seeing me off I got systematically, preposterously drunk. Even so, a weird lucidity possesses my memory of that afternoon: my girl Laurel, small, blond, elegantly shaped, respectably married (to a doctor), with whom I had worked out a warm alliance not lacking in tenderness but for the most part studiously carnal, sat snuggled next to me in the cool dark, biting her lips as she wondered about leaves, furloughs, weekends. The bar was milling with people, most of them talking too loud, and nearby I heard one man say to another: "The market's going to be in bad trouble if they de-escalate this war." I had not until that moment heard the verb "escalate," much less "de-escalate"—post-Hiroshima neologisms—and the word itself struck me as being some-how even more sordid than the sentiment which had just impelled its use.

But I had neared the point where I was past caring. Steadied by my mourning Laurel, I wobbled outside into the blinding light of Fifth Avenue. Front pages of the *Journal-American* sprouted everywhere—GOD BLESS GEN. MACARTHUR! the banner headlines read in feverish crimson—and it was not long before we saw the general himself: in an open Cadillac, flanked by shoals of motorcycle outriders, the ornate headpiece half an inch atilt as he saluted the mob with his corncob pipe, he fleetingly grimaced, gazing straight at me, and behind the raspberry-tinted sunglasses his eyes appeared as glassily opaque and mysterious as those of an old, sated lion pensively digesting a wildebeest or, more exactly, like those of a man whose thoughts had turned inward upon some Caesarean dream magnificent beyond compare. His glory worked like acid on my own sense of vulnerability. I was gripped by a feeling of doom and lonesomeness, and I think I stifled the urge to clout somebody when I heard a nearby voice say: "Hang that bastard Harry Truman!" In the taxi going to Penn Station I ignored the driver, who glanced at my uniform admiringly and called me a hero, and I paused only long enough to give Laurel a hot despairing kiss before plunging onto the train, where I slept stupefied all the way to Fredericksburg, Virginia.

The camp to which I had been ordered was originally known as New River. Then it later acquired the name Lejeune—after an illustrious marine commandant of a bygone era. Set amid the pinelands of the Carolina coast, the camp was still young as military establishments go; the next day when I arrived it was bustling and businesslike, as I always remembered it. I had spent a few tough months there during the previous war, and on the morning that I reported for duty I was stung by an awful sense of recollection at the sight of the broad asphalt avenues filled with marching men—along with that intimidating tramp of regimented feet that I thought I had put out of my ears for good—and by the vista of brick barracks and headquarters buildings with their phony Federalist cupolas so reminiscent of some callow newly built college campus almost anywhere in the nation. My emotions must have been very close to those of an ex-convict who has savored the sweet taste of liberty only to find himself once more a transgressor at the prison gates, gazing up at the long-familiar walls. It was unseasonably warm. The base had already changed over to khaki uniform and I felt in my green woolens not only awkward and conspicuous but near suffocation. I was also hungover, jittery with exhaustion, and gripped with such foreboding about the future that my mind retreated from all notion of what the next year or years might bring, and in my thoughts I fiddled with the past.

From the top-floor window of the administration building, where I stood smoking a cigarette, waiting for the division adjutant to receive me, I could see across miles of swampland—fiercely green now in the full tide of springtime—almost to the ocean. Cypress, scrub oak, palmetto, tupelo, and countless groves of longleaf pine—all watered by the estuarial marsh in which they spread their roots, and by evil, slow-running brown streams that had nearly drowned more than one wretched recruit: this was the wilderness which only ten years before the generals had surveyed from the air and, observing its proximity to the sea, had pronounced ideal for training young men in the new amphibious-warfare theory, or "doctrine," as it was known. Rugged and isolated, far removed from any metropolitan fleshpots, it was the perfect place to harden up troops for what turned out to be the cruelest combat ever known in the annals of war: it was lonely, inhospitable, frigid in winter, a steaming cauldron in summer, and largely uninhabited save for mosquitoes, ticks, and chiggers in stupendous numbers, possums, poisonous water moccasins, a few bobcats and bears, and, on the relatively dry periphery of the fastness, a tiny, scattered community of Negroes who scratched out a poor living on plots of tobacco and peanuts. These people— they had lived on the land for generations—had not been taken into much account by the generals during their aerial survey. As I stood there, I once again recalled hearing how half a dozen of the Negroes had killed themselves rather than face eviction—an outbreak of suicides that caused widespread talk in the region, especially since self-destruction, by the light of southern mythology, is rare among a race of people born to patiently endure their suffering.

But some had killed themselves, and those who survived them had been "equitably" paid and resettled, transported to another county. Behind them they left scattered along dusty tracks through the pinewoods a dilapidated hodgepodge of tobacco barns, sheds, privies, cabins, and a handful of cross-roads stores plastered with signs advertising RC Cola and Dr. Pepper and Copenhagen snuff. Windowless and abandoned, with porches rotting and tar-paper roofs in tatters, they sagged amid overgrown plots of sunflowers and weeds, or became carapaced in sweet jungles of honeysuckle where the drowsy hum of bees only made more pronounced the sense of a final silence of bereavement, of life stilled. Yet not without some value even in their utter desolation, the shacks and stores began to serve as objectives in field exercises, something to be captured; many more became targets for artillery and mortar practice, and as I gazed out over the green roof of the woods I remembered how on a hot summer day in 1944 my own platoon had laid down round after round of mortar fire upon one of these derelict shanties, firing for effect until our barrage had turned the place to splinters and nothingness save for a single crudely painted metal signboard that we discovered amid the wreckage, which read, WHITEHURST'S STORE. And I recalled feeling then a small tug at my heart, not for any damage done to an already ruined hulk, nor even out of conscience, but because Whitehurst was the name of my father's mother, whose family had lived here on this Carolina coast for two centuries and had owned Negroes who bore the Whitehurst name. Thus this storekeeper had most certainly been descended from slaves owned by my ancestors—could it be that he was one of those who had sought suicide in his grief? I never found out—and as I stood on that smoking ruin with its intermingled fragrance of gunpowder and honeysuckle I could not help but feel a pang of morbid regret over the fact that it was I who had presided so efficiently at the obliteration of a place one Whitehurst must have once cherished dearly. It seemed oddly gratuitous on my part, and something of an insult.

The assistant adjutant was a laconic, mistrustful-eyed major who dealt speedily with my suggestion that my talents might best be suited for the more demanding cerebral activities of the rear echelon—I had murmured something about "public relations"—and assigned me to the command of a mortar platoon in one of the infantry battalions. Later in the day, after reporting to my battalion office, I was shown the place where I would live during the next few months before shipping out to Korea: a room on the second floor of one of the several brick buildings that served as the Bachelor Officers' Quarters. The room, designed for occupancy by two persons, was airy enough and reasonably comfortable-looking, but both it and the quarters themselves—functional, institutional, with dark echoing corridors and a communal washroom filled with the sound of urinals in spasm, the whole place soupily miasmic from roaring showers—reminded me again painfully of college, of a dormitory, and I realized how truly retrogressive my life had become.

One facility possessed by this B.O.Q., however, which I had never seen in a college dormitory was a serious, full-sized bar fit for a modest hotel: here, where mixed drinks were twenty-five cents apiece (how seductively available are creature comforts in the military service, at least behind the front lines), the recalled reserve officers gathered each afternoon at five, uniforms abandoned, gaudy in sport shirts, drawn together by a camaraderie born in chagrin, resentment, homesickness, anxiety, and a common need to make heard the sound of distress. Certainly not even in the previous war was there ever such easy companionship, such a sense of a community of victims; and it was here at the Bachelor Officers' Quarters bar that we met most often that spring to discuss our woes. And it may have been that first day—surely it was no more than a couple of days later—that I made the acquaintance of Lacy Dunlop, who, like most of the Bachelor Officers, was no bachelor.

"Look at them," Lacy said to me, gesturing around the dark, murmurous room. "The fellowship of the damned. Did you know there's a new Chinese offensive expected at the Hwachon Reservoir? By fall I'll bet half of the poor sods in this place will have their asses shot off. And all because we signed that creepy little piece of paper."

"How long have you been here?" I asked.

"Oh hell, I got here the end of January. I drew a rifle platoon in the Sixth Marines. It was hell for a while. Sheer hell. Freezing cold, you can't imagine how cold it was out in the swamps. And here I was, hadn't touched a rifle in six years, and I was supposed to be leading a bunch of eighteen-year-old gung-ho kids just up from Parris Island. Oh Christ, it was awful, those field problems. Physically, I was a nasty old sponge. I'd forgotten how to read a map, and I was expected to be an *example*, you see, full of esprit de corps and all that silly crap." He paused and flipped into his mouth the olive from his martini glass. "Really, unless you were out in those swamps for six weeks in the winter you'll never understand how—well, I mean, *blissful* a spring like this can be."

From the jukebox, abruptly, there boomed forth the words of "My Truly, Truly Fair," causing me, unaccountably, to feel a sharp sense of imprisonment. When played in a martial setting, popular songs have a way of heightening one's mood of isolation: dealing with peaceable pursuits like ball games and courtship, they tend to sadden, and to mock one's ears. In the Second World War, this song for me was "Don't Fence Me In." Now I realized I had acquired another: "My Truly, Truly Fair," loud, lushly orchestrated, infinitely desolating. I would have settled for the *Missa Solemnis*.

"No, you see, ever since this stuff in Korea began, the poor old Corps has had to readjust its thinking," Lacy went on. "Marines before this were always snooping and pooping in the jungle, you know, chasing the Japs in the Pacific or working for Wall Street in Haiti and Nicaragua. Most all of the marine wars have been tropical wars. But after last winter and that ghastly retreat from the Chosin Reservoir, with all those poor guys freezing their peckers off, the brass has gotten what they like to call 'winter-oriented' in their thinking—isn't that an exquisite phrase?—which means that my battalion commander, guy named Hudson who is very shot in the ass with the Corps anyway, made a *fetish* of walking us through as many frozen creeks as he could find. Oh, my friend, April is the least cruel month I know, and you should count your blessings for getting here now."

"When do you think we'll be shipping out overseas?" I asked.

"Oh, I don't know. No one seems to know. But the best guess is that we'll be here at least until midsummer. God, I hope it's not too soon, or ever. We've *had* our war, for Christ's sake. I've had enough of this bullshit mucking about in the Orient."

As it turned out, I got to know Lacy Dunlop better than any of my fellow reserve officers; in fact, we struck up a sympathetic and animated friendship, having more than our unprosperous future in common. Lacy was a few years older than I—he was twenty-eight or twenty-nine—though he had the blue-eyed, blond, snub-nosed good looks that gave him the appearance of a teenager; at first glance there had been something almost ridiculously regular and conventional about his open, boyish face—I thought of the well-scrubbed American kid in the Coca-Cola and hair-tonic ads—but the impression of unsoiled youth he made was largely superficial, a cosmetic accident: beneath the fresh fraternity-boy countenance lay a temper that was experienced, complicated, sardonic, and wise. Much of this had been acquired at the hard business of war. While barely twenty he had been commissioned a second lieutenant, and had participated as

a platoon commander in some of the most ferocious engage-
ments on Okinawa, coming out of it unharmed but with
somber memories of those who had been slaughtered all
around him—"like termites," he said.

After the war he finished up at Columbia, in the city of
his birth, taking a degree in philosophy. Later he went to
France, where he studied at the Sorbonne, married a French
girl, and where—possessed by the same "lunacy," as he put
it, that had affected everyone else—he succumbed to the
fatal invitation to rejoin the reserves. Shortly after this he received news of the death of his father, the patriarch of an old
Westchester WASP family and the publisher of a small but
prosperous list of scientific textbooks, and Lacy returned to
New York with his French bride in order to take over the firm
and to live a civilized life made up of "good wine, good books
and music, orderly children, and two months in France
every summer." But this fantasy had been blown to pieces.
As for his present plight, he had faced it neither with sulky
rebelliousness, as a few had, nor with supine acceptance, as
had some others, but with a kind of controlled and cynical
desperation permeated by grisly good humor. About the only
truly solemn fear I ever heard him give voice to was that he
might get killed without making, with his wife Annie, another summer visit to the small farmhouse he had bought in
the hills near Grasse.

"Of course, you understand there are degrees of misery,"
he went on, "and if you are attentive to this fact it will allow
you a certain consolation, if only in a relative way. For instance, take your own situation. On an ascending scale of
misery, from one to ten, I'd place you around one, or a little
less. Why? Well look, in the first place you're not married,

you have no responsibilities or financial obligations, no one to support, so basically your misery index is insignificant. It's true you're not getting a regular piece of ass but, *tant pis,* which of us is? At least you've gotten your book written and can hope for some small immortality, also a bit of money, if you live that long. Then too, remember that you're an officer and, compared to these enlisted reserves, you get to live with some of the amenities. So I'd place you almost as far down on the misery scale as it's possible to get."

"Where would you put yourself, smart guy?" I said. The twenty-five-cent bourbon had filled me with a soothing melancholy, and Lacy's game caused me to float between distant annoyance and straightforward fascination. "Nine? Or ten?"

"Oh God, no. Misery-wise, I don't claim any points. I do have the responsibility of a wife, which puts me ahead of you a bit. And because the housing situation here makes her have to stay in New York, that gives me another small notch. But we have no children—blind chance, but fortunate under the circumstances—and in addition I have a good solid professional who's running the family business, and it continues to make money nicely in my absence. It would be swinishly presumptuous of me to put my misery any higher than two or three, miserable though I am."

The bar had begun to fill up with officers—young fellows between twenty-five and thirty-five mostly, lieutenants and captains in sport shirts and slacks, save for a sprinkling of grimy types in green dungarees just in from some field problem, sweatily gulping cans of beer. In twos or threes, in clusters of a half dozen or more, they lolled around the perfunctory Formica tables or stood restlessly at the bar itself as their voices, not loud but very urgent, filled the air with a passionate monotone of discontent. Sometimes I heard laughter but it sounded bitter, and it was more often than not cut off short, as if whoever had laughed had sensed an impropriety. I was struck by the ease with which I was soon able to distinguish the newcomers like myself from those who had shared with Lacy the routine of several months. The veterans, besides being trimmer and tanner, seemed to bear themselves with a certain casual, glum assurance, as if they had become acclimated to the stress of this new existence, had through slow reacquaintance become finally adjusted to once familiar duties and tensions; their faces wore looks of bemused resignation, and they appeared older than their years. The recent arrivals, most of whom were sallow of hue and who were puffed out in places with telltale sedentary flab, put me in mind of new boys at summer camp—chafing with homesickness, eyes roving in quest of friendship, altogether unstrung.

But whatever our situation, we were all bound to each other by a single shocked awareness, and this was that for the second time in less than a decade we were faced with the prospect of an ugly death. In an abstract way it was possible to say that it was our own fault we were here. Yet suddenly, as my gaze wandered from face to face among this sullen, murmurous assembly of misplaced civilians—these store owners and office managers and personnel directors and salesmen—I was gripped by a foreboding about our presence in this swampy wilderness that at once transcended and made absurd each of our individual destinies, and even our collective fate. For it seemed to me that all of us were both exemplars and victims of some uncontrollable aggres-

sion, a hungry will for bloodshed creeping not only throughout America but the world, and I could not help but abruptly
shiver in that knowledge.

I recall having felt sleepy and in need of a nap before
dinner, and I'd arisen to go to my room upstairs when Lacy
put a hand on my arm and said: "There are many fives and
sixes and sevens on the misery scale—chaps with lots of
kids, and those who've had to lose their jobs, and combina-
tions of these. They have misery aplenty. But there are only
a few authentic nines and tens. Look over there if you want
to see Mr. Misery himself."

Morose and balding, a mesomorph of thirty with well-
developed biceps, thick wrists, and wire-rimmed spectacles
that made him look disarmingly professorial, Mr. Misery sat
with a single companion at a nearby table, sunk in obvious
despair. He had a large, dark drink before him and it was
clear that he had worked his way through many others.

"The guy's name is Phil Santana, whom you might have
heard of if you read the sports pages. He was a big amateur
golfer a few years ago, won several famous championships,
and then became a pro. He caught a lot of shit on Iwo, last
war. A captain. Wife and three kids, was a pro at some fancy
club near Cleveland and owned a very successful golf shop.
A chap like that, his livelihood depends almost entirely on
his direct, personal contact with people. He can't leave it to
someone else to run. It took him three or four rather strenuous years to build up the kind of business he had, and once
he leaves it the whole thing dissolves—a bubble, finished.
But he had to sell out, poor joker. I truly pity him."

"What's he going to do?" I asked.

"There's only one thing he can do now," Lacy said. "And

that's to ship over into the regular marines—for life. And that's what he told me that he's sure he's going to have to do."

I was silent for a long moment, brooding on this Procrustean fable. Then I said: "That's terrible. That's just terrible." I meant it.

"Fortunes of war," said Lacy.

I excused myself and rose to go, just as the jukebox exploded again into life, a garish, winking rainbow, and "My Truly, Truly Fair" filled the bar with its synthetic rapture. I had a last glimpse of the ex–golf pro, whose face—bereft and etched with panic—seemed for an instant to make incarnate the mood of each man in the forlorn, oppressive, temporary room.

II

One afternoon about three weeks later I had my first encounter with Paul Marriott. The occasion was a uniformed cocktail party—a "wetting down"—at the main officers' club given by Lacy's battalion executive officer, a regular who had just been promoted from captain to major. I didn't know the new major; in fact, I had gotten to know few regular officers, sidestepping them as everyone else did during after-duty hours. There was, I suppose, little of what might be termed hostility existing between us reserves and the professional officers—the demands of order and discipline precluded that—but we did regard each other with mild constraint and as if by unspoken agreement tended to observe a good-natured social apartheid, as white folks and Negroes do in certain genteel towns of the South.

In addition to a philosophical opposition—anti-war in nature—that already existed among us, our civilian days had prevented most of us from having anything in common with the regulars. They were all wrapped up in their training manuals and tables of organization and their dreams of advancement. As for ourselves, it would have required an almost total absence of perception on the part of the career officers not to be aware of our half-buried rage and bitterness. So after five in the afternoon we drifted apart—they to their wives and their lawn sprinklers and their custom kitchens in the spruce bungalows off base, we to the seething barrios of our B.O.Q.s, where we could scheme and bitch to our hearts' content.

For some reason—perhaps because of his longer, tougher experience in the Pacific, which gave him a little more sense of solidarity with the professionals—Lacy was one of the few reserves who seemed to be able to move at ease in either camp. Since I'd first met him, he had talked to me at length about the officer class newly emergent after World War II, which he saw as a sinister development in the national life. He confided to me that he was both fascinated and amused by these men—by their style and by their strangely oblique, arcane vocabulary, above all by their hectic ambition (though he was not so amused at this)—and he felt himself a spy among them, gathering notes on the genesis of some as yet dimly conceived apocalypse. At any rate, when he asked me to go along with him to the party for the newborn major I readily agreed, infected by his own spirit of research.

"The book reads wonderfully well so far," Lacy said to me as we drove out to the officers' club in his car, a low black Citroën he had brought back from France. It was that famous standard model from back in the 1930s, now defunct, with the long, arrogant hood and flaring fenders—the first one that I or, for that matter, practically anyone else in post-war America had ever seen—and its slinky Gallic panache here on the base among so many Fords and Oldsmobiles had caused more than one glance of suspicion. "I'm really impressed by the book, you know," he went on. "When do I get to look at another installment?"

I had been receiving, piecemeal, galley proofs of my novel, which Lacy had asked to read. Save for Laurel, one or two friends in New York, and a few people at the publishing house, Lacy was the first to set eyes on my inaugural work. I had sensed in him by now an exceptional delicacy and discrimination in literary matters—also a winning honesty. I was eager for his praise, and when it came it warmed and touched me. I mumbled my appreciation.

"Say, incidentally, there's someone else who wants to see the galleys, if you can manage it. Can I show them to him?" he said.

"Who's that?" I asked.

"My battalion commander, the new one I told you about. The one who replaced Boondock Ben Hudson. He just took over, though I've seen a lot of him before."

"You must be kidding," I said, looking at him. "A *battalion commander*? Reading my southern gothic romance? You've gone completely out of your mind."

"No sir," he replied with a smile. "It's true, I mean it." He paused, then added: "Well, you'll see."

Although we were late, the cocktail party was still in progress when we arrived at the officers' club. With its sparkling swimming pool and canopied entrance, its restaurant, its elephantine bar, and its overall feeling of catered leisure, the club was a place I had come to rather intensely dislike. I preferred by far the sensible, lumpen utility of the B.O.Q. bar (at least you could curse the Marine Corps there) to this vulgar hybrid—part country club, part luxury hotel—which seemed so cheap a simulacrum of a true elegance to be found in the outside world, and where one dared not utter a word against military life. Pompous murals were everywhere, as intimidating as those in a Moscow subway station, proclaiming Marine Corps victories of yesteryear—Tripoli, Belleau Wood, Iwo Jima—and so in this pleasure dome made for relaxation I could not relax but was forever squirming with premonitions of a garish future mural, titled *Korea,* with myself among the fallen martyrs. The entire club had about it an aroma of gin, brass polish, Arpège, and grilled sirloin; it left me troubled by its atmosphere—both muscular and oddly feminine—of vapid affluence.

"Check that," Lacy murmured as we mounted the front steps.

At the side of a major directly in front of us, a long-legged blond girl with one of the finest, firmest bottoms I ever beheld slithered with a delicious little giggle through the open door, hair suddenly atumble and golden on an air-conditioned breeze. Her angular, scowling escort, plainly a regular, wore campaign ribbons up to his clavicle, and looked like a creep. They both vanished.

"Jesus," said Lacy. My heart was instantly roiling with hatred, envy, and lust.

"I'd like to—" I began, wildly distracted, twenty-six years old, an about-to-be-successful writer in the full bloom of his youthful virility and allure—doomed to this continence, this stupid banishment.

"Now, now," Lacy put in, "it is strictly forbidden to handle the merchandise."

I knew how right he was. Because of the housing shortage, nearly all of the married reserves had been forced to leave their wives at home, while bachelors like myself were set adrift to lick their chops over the handful of lady marines on the base or to make abortive forays among the navy nurses, most of whom were either bony or fat. It was the regulars who had the women. Though I'm sure it was an illusion, each of them seemed to be southern—glossy little china figurines with roseate cheeks and vacant eyes, created from the same mold. Southern-born myself, I had learned to mistrust them. Thirtyish, sexy in a dimly flirtatious, untouchable Dixieland way, they were filled with dumb talk about leaves and transfers and promotions, or about the music of Lawrence Welk or the comparative merits of the PX at Quantico and Camp Pendleton and "Pearl." Most of them dawdled through the late-spring days beside the club swimming pool, where they nibbled on ice-cream bars and read *Leatherneck* and *Reader's Digest* and played canasta. One such regular officer's wife—odorous of gardenia and with splendid breasts swelling beneath a low-cut blouse— spoke to me as we stood, drinks in hand, next to a gory frieze of cockaded marines storming the Mexican redoubt at Chapultepec. She asked me if my novel—which Lacy had told her about—was fiction or nonfiction.

"That's a crazy question, honey," said her husband, a chunky captain from Georgia, rather snappishly. "A novel *has* to be fiction. That's the definition of a novel."

The girl blushed deeply, then said, "Oh, I know that. What I guess I really mean is, what's the story about?"

"So you're a scrivener?" the captain persisted. "Imagine

having a real live scrivener down here in the boondocks. Well, we get all kinds these days. Over in the Eighth Marines the other day they got a hairdresser, I mean a guy who actually *does* women's hair." My heart shriveled. His voice was amiable enough, its tone told me that he meant no sarcasm, and I'm certain that he was as ignorant as I was then of the definition of the word scrivener ("an author who is either minor or unknown," true enough in my case). But there was a planetary distance between our two worlds and I wished he would get off the subject of my novel, about which he now inquired: "Is it psychological or historical?"

"It's about group sex," Lacy volunteered. And that was a fairly daring thing to say in 1951, among strangers and in mixed company at that. The captain flinched, his wife flushed pink again, and for an instant the spirit of Southern Baptist rectitude seemed to attend us like a tormented presence. But then the silence was broken by a voice at Lacy's side, addressing him in melodious, unaccented French: "*Bonsoir, bonsoir, mon vieux. Comment ça va? Où étiez-vous? Je vous ai cherché partout. Êtes-vous là depuis longtemps?*"

"*Bonsoir, mon colonel,*" Lacy replied. "*Ça va bien, et vous? Non, nous venons juste d'arriver.* Colonel, I'd like you to meet a friend of mine." Then he turned and I was introduced to Lieutenant-Colonel Paul Marriott, United States Marine Corps.

"So you're the writer Lacy's been telling me about?" he said pleasantly. The way he pronounced "about"—making it rhyme with "boot"—told me he was a Virginian. "Well, it's refreshing to have a literary man around. It adds a needed dash of variety, and I hope we can have a talk or two. . . . I'd like you gentlemen to meet my son Mike."

It generally strikes me as an affectation when people

speak in French if there is no particular reason to do so, but both Lacy and the colonel were very fluent—the colonel, to my ear, practically flawless—and this, together with a slight tone of self-mockery, made it attractively droll. As for the colonel himself, I could not help being almost overwhelmed by his ribbons and decorations: if important enough, and if present in sufficient numbers, their luster does tend at immediate sight to dominate the image, and to outshine the face of their owner. Yet it was not just the magnitude of the decorations themselves that was so impressive (the Navy Cross *and* the Silver Star—each indicating an exploit of what must have been hair-raising valor—in addition to a Legion of Merit and a Purple Heart with stars denoting several wounds), but the dazzling collage of campaign and expeditionary ribbons and marksmanship awards which went along with them, and which could only be worn by a man whose life had been bound up with the marines since early youth. I was in the presence, I reflected, of an absolute professional. Even so, Colonel Marriott looked and (as I later learned) was barely past forty: it sharpened the contradiction between this spangled testimony to a career busily devoted to the arts of war and his worldly, cultivated manner. How, I wondered, had such a relatively young man lived a life so rich in military fulfillment yet found the time to become expert in another language and, presumably, to develop a taste for the Finer Things?

I shook hands with the colonel's son—a boy of about eighteen who greatly resembled his father. Except for the obvious difference in their ages, and the fact that he was a shade taller, he could almost have passed for his father's twin—which is to say that like his parent he was of medium height and athletically built (without, however, appearing aggressively muscled) and like him, too, had cropped sandy hair and intelligent eyes set deeply in a cleanly sculpted face. Despite this likeness, however, the lad had no intention of following his father's career: that I learned soon after being introduced when, as Lacy and the colonel chatted, I asked him whether he was going to be a professional marine. I don't know why I posed the question; perhaps the extraordinary resemblance made it seem inevitable.

"Lord no," he replied in a soft voice. "I don't want to hurt anyone." The response caused my scalp to prickle, largely because of its level frankness, devoid of any sardonic edge. He looked vaguely unhappy, a bit restless. Shifting my tack, I learned that he was a sophomore at Chapel Hill and that he hoped one day to be an architect. Suddenly his face crinkled up in a smile. "I think I'd rather sell hot dogs than be in the marines. If I ever get drafted I'll do my bit in the air force."

I had no more time to pursue the reasons for this mysterious stance, for just at that moment the colonel suggested that we join him at a nearby table. A buffet supper was to be served later, and as we seated ourselves the sound of dance music erupted in a distant room, washing over us with the muffled din of trombones and clarinets; softly overtaking me, a liquor-warm mood of felicity closed round my senses like the inside of some large, benign fist, lulling me into a deceptive feeling of peace. It grew dark outside; the swimming pool and the escarpment of pine trees behind it were drowned in shadows. The war seemed far away, and for the first time since my arrival in camp I felt positively buoyed by alcohol, rather than having it feed and aggravate my discontent. Beyond any doubt it was Colonel Marriott who was responsible for this gentle euphoria: that the Marine Corps contained one regular officer capable of such enlightened, original conversation was enough to make me want to revise entirely my jaundiced estimate of military life. And although I recollect our talk as being "literary" (at twenty-six I doted on such earnest discourse), I found the colonel unpretentiously knowledgeable—astonishing me all the more since pretentiousness in matters they know little about is a common trait among career officers, especially those above the rank of captain. But even before this I was taken with him; he displayed a sympathy for my predicament that was quite out of the ordinary.

"It must have been one hell of a wrench for you," he said, "enough to put one into a state of shock. Especially when you have this book coming out. But I suspect you've fallen into the routine by now. Are things very much different from '45?"

"Well, very much the same," I replied, "some things a little better—the chow, for example." And this was, I had to confess to myself, substantially true. Although hardly a culinary miracle, the food was infinitely more palatable than the revolting swill we had been fed much of the time in the previous war. "I mean, over at the B.O.Q. the other evening I had some roast beef that was really first-rate."

The colonel smiled. The easy informality he encouraged had caused me already to drop the "sir," which ordinarily I might have continued to use until we were much better acquainted. Also, I took the cue from Lacy, whom I had heard once call him "Paul."

"Yes," he said, "the Old Corps is shaping up in many remarkable ways. Food for years and years was one area in which the Corps was glaringly behind the navy. I've contended all along that with excellent raw material available there was no reason in the world why the food for both officers and men couldn't be considerably more than just edible, and that our mess halls could turn out some really civilized meals. Well, somehow, someone got the message a year or so ago, and the cooking's not half bad now. Say, tell me," he interrupted himself, obviously wanting to change the subject, "what about this book of yours? Lacy's very excited about what he's read. He says it's bound to cause a big stir when it comes out."

He asked me the publication date, and this led to a chatty discussion of books in general. The subject of literary influences came up and when I admitted, a bit awkwardly, that I feared that my work still betrayed rhythms and echoes of my predecessors—mainly Faulkner and Fitzgerald—he looked amused and said: "Oh hell, I wouldn't worry about that. It's impossible to be one hundred percent original. A writer *has* to be influenced by someone. Where would Faulkner be without Joyce, after all? Or take *From Here to Eternity*, have you read it?" Of course I had, everyone had; at that moment it was still a rampaging best seller. "It's one hell of a book, really. He's a mean bastard when he deals with the officers, but it's true enough. The influences are everywhere—Hemingway, Dreiser, Wolfe, the lot—but somehow it just doesn't matter. The book has a power that absorbs and transcends the influences."

At some point one of us spoke of Flaubert, and when I expressed my great admiration for his work the colonel said: "Well, if he's your man you really must read Steegmuller's book, if you haven't already."

"No, I'm afraid I haven't," I replied.

"Well, I really recommend *Flaubert and Madame Bovary,* a truly fascinating work. I'll lend you my copy if you can't get hold of one. By the way, do you read French?"

"Fairly well," I said, "for newspapers and magazines and such. But not well enough for a book like *Bovary.*"

"That's unfortunate, because of course it's written in the most, well—crystalline style imaginable. I imagine you've read the Aveling translation."

"Yes, that's the one."

"She's not at all bad, actually—certainly it'll do well enough until a better one comes along. A remarkable woman, you know. Did you know that she was the daughter of Karl Marx?"

"No, I didn't," I said with honest amazement. "That's fascinating. I just hadn't made the connection."

"Yes, and another strange thing about her—she was rather badly unbalanced mentally and finally became totally obsessed by the life of Bovary, by the career of this woman she'd rendered into English. Finally she killed herself and in the identical manner of Emma Bovary—by taking poison. It's one of the most curious tales in the history of literature."

I was at that time, indeed, especially devoted to Flaubert, and had been through *Bovary* so often that there were many passages which I had all but committed to memory. I had also read as much about the man's life as I could lay hands on (my failure to know about Steegmuller's book is an unexplainable mystery): Flaubert's enormous craft, his monkish dedication, his irony, his painstaking regard for the nuances of language—all of these commanded my passionate admiration. Few others shared room with Flaubert in my private pantheon of writers. I remember being seized by a vivid excitement as Paul (it was not "Paul" yet, but it later became so, and I'll refer to him this way hereafter) spoke of the master, alluding not only to his work, about which he seemed to know a great deal, but to his life—here he was equally well-informed. Although he was clearly a Flaubert votary like me, he had a wide-ranging knowledge of French literature in general, and the references he made to Maupassant, Zola, Turgenev, Daudet, and other of Flaubert's friends and contemporaries were pertinent, illuminating, and thoroughly grounded in broad reading. We had particular fun exchanging views on Louise Colet, Flaubert's mistress, speculating on her jealousy and her tantrums, and when I suggested that it was Flaubert's mother who was at the root of his neurosis and his flight from women, Paul paid tribute to my insight—which may not have been original—by saying: "Oh there's no doubt that you're absolutely right. It's straight out of the Freudian textbook. But at the same time Louise must have been an awful ball-breaker."

A pretty girl of seventeen or eighteen with red hair approached the table and Paul's son rose to greet her. Then the rest of us got up and, after introductions and a few murmured amenities, the boy and the girl bade us good night and left gaily, arm in arm. The interruption made me suddenly aware of how quickly the time had passed—outside it was dark and frogs madly piped in the swamp, numberless and shrill above the sound close by of a bleating saxophone. But this interlude had also brought me quickly back to earth; something had caused my wonderful mood to snap in two, and as I took my seat again I saw that Paul Marriott, like the prince transformed into baser stuff at one stroke of the wand, was once again a mere lieutenant-colonel, and the full panoply of stars and ribbons—miraculously lost to sight during the course of our dialogue—was now intimidatingly luminous across the robust chest. Lacy bent forward across the table to ask Paul about some coming field problem. As he did so, I was belatedly overcome by a kind of tickled, boozy wonderment over the fact that for more than an hour I had been engaged in a delicately articulated, absorbing, even scholarly conversation not with a literary critic, not with some rarefied denizen of an academic tower nor even the kind of bright dilettante one is likely to meet on a long ocean voyage but somebody else: a man of formidable experience who had managed to find in the muted and lilac-scented province of nineteenth-century France harmonies that were compatible with a career in the deafening, bloody universe of modern warfare. It was quite difficult to believe, but then again, I thought, maybe I was always too quick to sell the Marine Corps short.

The heat was fierce that summer; actually, it was sometimes beyond belief, surpassed reason. Situated as we were on the periphery of a vast swamp, the marines at the camp suffered as much from the humidity as from the sun, so that on certain awful days the effect was that of an inhuman steam bath which one could not turn off or escape from. One simply gasped, and groaned, and felt one's khakis or dungarees become limply awash, like wet flour sacks, the instant one put them on. It was bad enough out in the field; there we hiked and hustled under the baking sun, maneuvered in the woods, set up mortar positions in stifling gullies, and more than one of my boys had to be carried off to the infirmary, alarmingly dehydrated and in the near coma of heat-stroke. But out of doors there was often some relief: the shade of the trees offered protection now and then, a sudden breeze might surprise us with its fresh and cooling breath, and everywhere there were tidal streams to swim in. It was back at the main base, in the unventilated confines of the squat brick building which served as battalion headquarters, that the heat became insufferable, past description, so that I could compare it to nothing in my experience and was reminded only of legends I had once read concerning the boiling and benighted city of Villahermosa, in the tropical Mexican state of Tabasco, where even priests went mad with the heat and died railing at a deity heartless enough to create this inferno on earth. There at the office I was forced periodically to spend a morning or an afternoon hunched over a desk, where I would whimperingly go through the motions of some necessary paperwork and swill numberless Coca-Colas, and sweatily absorb for the fourth or fifth time my most recent letter from Laurel, all horny and asprawl upon Fire Island's halcyon strand.

It was after one such session, on a day in late June, that I made my troubled way back to the B.O.Q. Having risen at dawn, I thought I would take a nap before lunch and then go out to join my company in its training area. While I was climbing the stairs to my floor, I heard the sound of hillbilly music coming from a radio or phonograph, a raucous female plaint overlaid with a lot of corny fiddles and electronic vibrato, the entire racket far too loud and certainly an affront to the decorum of an officers' quarters, even though at the moment the place was virtually deserted.

Now, quite seriously I pride myself even today on having

been an early devotee of country music, which has only recently come into its own and earned some respectful attention from musical annotators. Perhaps one has to be southern-born to truly appreciate this homely, untamed genre, but from the time I was a boy I found in the music, at its best, a woebegone loveliness and simplicity of utterance, a balladry—sometimes wrenchingly haunting and sad—that was an authentic echo of the poor soil from which it had sprung, and I cannot even now hear the voices of Ernest Tubb or Roy Acuff or the Carter Family or Kitty Wells without being torn headlong from my surroundings and into a brief bittersweet vision of the pine forests and red earth, the backwoods stores and sluggish tidewater rivers, the whole tormented landscape of that strange world below the Potomac and north of the Rio Grande. But all art forms, of course, generate subforms that are debased and bastardized versions of the original—for every Beethoven ten Karl Goldmarks, for each *Messiah*, two dozen *Dreams of Gerontius*—and country music is no exception. At its worst—usually found in its scherzo mood—it is an abomination of synthetic rhythms and bumpkin lyrics, all of it glutinously orchestrated with cellos, vibraphones, electric organs, and God knows what other instruments formerly undreamed of in the Great Smokies or on the banks of the Apalachicola. It was this kind of music I heard as I gained the landing on my floor, realizing, half-deafened and astonished, that it was emanating from my own room.

Ding-dong Daddy, whatcha doin' to me—

I had become spoiled. Having lived for weeks as the sole occupant of a room designed for two, I had all but forgotten the possibility of a roommate—who plainly had just moved in. As a matter of fact, his efficiency was such that he had already been inspired to add his name to the card on the frame of the door, and below my name had neatly printed his identification:

SECOND LT. DARLING P. JEETER, JR., USMC

Bemused, I gazed at the card for some time, struck by the cadence of the name itself, which I tested several times on palate and tongue, but also by the absence, at the end of "USMC," of an "R," designating a reserve. And my spirits sank as I realized that come what may I had drawn a regular. I opened the door, the music boomed forth:

Ding-dong Daddy, whatcha doin' to me—
Had me jumpin' an' a-humpin' till half past three—

And I beheld, seated at the desk naked but for his green skivvy drawers, stamping out time to the cretinous song with bare feet, a stocky, muscular young man of twenty-one or twenty-two with acne scars on his cheeks and shoulders, wire-rimmed spectacles, straw-colored hair clipped to a half-inch skinhead cut, and—largely due to a wet, protuberant lower lip and an exceptionally meager forehead—an expression of radiant vacuity. If this description seems more than reasonably unfavorable, it is because I mean it to be, since nothing my roommate did or said during the course of our acquaintanceship diminished that first impression of almost unprecedented loutishness.

"Howdy," he said, rising and turning down his phonograph, coming forward to shake my hand. I noticed that he had pushed the proofs of my novel somewhat aside on the desk, also my dictionary and several other of the few books I had brought with me—Oscar Williams's modern American

verse anthology and the Viking *Portable Dante* were two I remember—and these now shared space with a mountainous
pile of phonograph records, presumably of the order of
"Ding-dong Daddy," three long, unsheathed, murderous-
looking blue-steel knives, a stack of "men's" magazines
(*True, Argosy,* and the like), a box of Baby Ruth candy bars,
and a random assortment of toilet articles including, I could
not help but notice, a large cellophane-wrapped pack of
fancy condoms known as "wet skins."

He gave me a firm grip. "Name's Darling Jeeter," he de-
clared in a hearty voice, clearly that of an Ole Country Boy.
"Muh friends all call me Dee."

I was relieved that he so quickly took care of the name
business (he must have had the problem before) since had
he not offered me the way out I was prepared to say politely
and immediately: "I'm very sorry but I cannot possibly call
you Darling." For although the patronymic is certainly ven-
erable enough (was it mere whimsy that led Barrie to give
that honored name to the family in *Peter Pan?*), and although to christen one's offspring with a family name is a
common enough practice throughout the South (my roommate, as it turned out, hailed from down in Florence, South
Carolina), I considered myself already too sensitive to this
new and, on my part, desperately unwanted intimacy to com-
pound my discomfort by having to say things like "Darling,
would you mind handing me the soap?" or, God forbid . . .
well, the possibilities were too numerous to contemplate.

Anyway, I introduced myself to Dee, and while I was
groggy with the need for a short nap, I felt it only proper that
the two of us—officers, gentlemen, southerners at that—sit
down and at least go through the motions of getting acquainted, especially when it looked as if we were destined to

be cheek by jowl for some time that summer in a climate not really suited for harmonious relations at close quarters. Dee, as it turned out, was a hand-to-hand-combat expert, his specialty knife fighting "close in"; the reason I had enjoyed several weeks of grace without his company was because this period he had spent in California, at the marine base at Camp Pendleton, where he had learned all the tricks of his trade. He had been sent back to Lejeune as an instructor, and was looking forward enormously to his vocation, brief as he hoped it would be.

"I'll go anywhere the Corps sends me, that's muh duty you see, but if you want to know the God-durn real truth what I really want to do is get over to Korea and stick about six inches of cold steel in as many of those God-durned gooks I can get holt of."

"How long have you been in the Corps?" I asked.

"Nine months and eight days," he replied. "I was in ROTC"—he pronounced it "Rotacy"—"at Clemson and then I took a commission and they done sent me to Quantico. Couldn't fire a rifle worth a shit on account of muh eyes"— he gestured toward his spectacles, and peered out at me from behind them with an expression that seemed peculiarly faraway and dim, like a rodent's, not aglint with the fervor of a knife fighter but somehow mossed over with the glaze of arrested development, or perhaps only fifteen years or so of slow fruition in the schools of South Carolina—"but I got me a waiver on the eyes, and I volunteered for knife fightin', which is the thing I truly come to love. Sometimes I think that a knife is the God-durned prettiest thing in the world. Stick that ole thing in, twist an' shove, twist an' shove—shee-it, man! Care for some pogey bait?"

Not since my early days in the Corps in World War II

had I heard the words "pogey bait"—old-time marine and navy slang for candy—and as he reached for the box of Baby Ruths I declined, saying that the weather was too hot and that, besides, my stomach felt rather poorly. Most of the reserves had made a point, generally, of *not* using the accepted seagoing vocabulary; I soon learned that Dee employed a salty locution whenever possible—"deck" for "floor," "bulkhead" for "wall"—which did little to further weld our relationship.

"Ordinarily," he went on, "I relish an Almond Joy or two along about this time of the morning, but the PX run out of Joys. Had to settle for the Ruths."

"Tell me," I said, honestly curious, "have you ever killed anybody with one of those knives?"

He took the question with equanimity. "Naw," he replied, "at Pendleton we practiced on dummies—and on each other, but with rubber blades. Naw, I ain't killed anybody *yet*—I'll have to confess."

I could not help but pursue the tack I had embarked upon and I said: "Dee, listen, don't you think *killing* people with a knife might just *sicken* you? I mean, just to watch some guy's guts fall out, and the blood and everything—well, I know knife fighting is sometimes necessary and damned useful when the chips are down, but Jesus, how can you actually think you're going to *like* it?" He had gnawed off the end of a Baby Ruth and was masticating it thoughtfully; the candy was sweetly odorous on the close hot air, and for an instant, vaguely nauseated, I was borne away in a queasy trance of chocolate, peanuts, vanillin, lecithin, hydrogenated vegetable oil, emulsifiers. A runnel of sweat made its way down his hairless belly which, like the rest of him, seemed as tight as rawhide despite his confectionery yen. I lusted for sleep, felt my eyelids slide closed, and listened to a cicada's shrill crickety screech, electric against the eardrum, as it scraped somewhere outside in the lowering heat.

"Well you see, ordinarily I might get sick like you say," he replied. "I don't truly like the sight of blood any more than the next man. But this here is a different matter now. We face the greatest peril this country has ever known. Did you see that movie they shown us at Pendleton? *Red Evil on the Earth* it was called, somethin' like that, about how those Communist bastards are takin' over everywhere. Sons of bitches. Guy with the bushy beard—what's his name?— Marx, and that other Russian son of a bitch, I forget his name, the bald one with that itty-bitty goatee on him like a streak of dog doo, God durn, boy, let me get a knife into both of them Communist sons of bitches, twist an' shove, twist an' shove, that's all, and you'll figure out pretty quick how a man can love cold steel."

"They're both already dead," I said.

"They're both dead, all righty-dighty," he said evenly. "Then I'll kill some other good Communist son of a bitch, preferably the color of yellow. You know what the only good kind of Communist there is, don't you?"

"Yes," I said, "a dead one. Look, Dee, I was up at four this morning and I'm terribly tired. I wonder if you'd mind shutting off the music for a while and let me take a little nap."

"Shore," he replied, "you go right ahead. I'll just be real quiet and put muh gear away. You go on and have you some good sack duty while ole Dee gets things squared away."

As I was drifting off I heard him say: "How do you figure the situation shapes up for a little nooky around here?"

"A few navy nurses, Dee," I murmured, "that's all. O.K. if you like them real big. Or short and scrawny."

"Shee-it, man," I heard him say, far off through the misty onset of slumber, "I love nooky any which way. I'm just like muh ole daddy. If I could find me a pussy big enough I'd set up camp inside—mess tents, flagpole, parade ground and all."

Dee's connection with his daddy was, as it turned out, neither casual nor merely reminiscent. When I returned to the B.O.Q. the next morning after spending a night in the field, Dee and his father were sitting at the desk munching on Almond Joys. The elder Jeeter was a man in what I took to be his late fifties or early sixties, haggard-looking with a pale, sad, gentle face deeply furrowed and lined; even at my first glance I saw that he was desperately sick. He wore an imitation pongee sport shirt through which a few old chalky-white hairs poked limply, and sacklike trousers, rather wrinkled and dirty, of a defeated greenish hue. He smelled mysteriously of something bitter and metallic, and was seized now and then by a horrible racking cough; I could recall no one for whose health on so short an acquaintance I felt such immediate alarm. He called Dee "Juney." A one-time Gunner—the marine term for warrant officer—he had served in the Corps for thirty-five years and had just come up from Florence to visit his newly commissioned son. He was a widower.

"What do you do on the outside, son?" the retired Gunner inquired of me in a kindly voice. Like Jeeter junior he spoke in a rich, loamy, Low Country drawl, with overtones of that arcane South Carolina dialect called Geechee. He sucked tirelessly at cigarettes.

"I'm a writer," I replied.

"You work around hosses?" he went on pleasantly.

"Not rider," I said sharply, "writer. I'm a writer. I write books. Prose. Prose fiction. What the French call *romans*." My sarcasm was heavy and intentional. A blaze of rage flared up behind my eyes, prompted in part by the Gunner's well-meaning density but also because of the sense of crowdedness the room suddenly gave me—cramped enough with two persons, it was made to seem positively thronged by the presence of a third—and because of my despair over new rumors that we were soon to ship out for Korea and by a general sense of doom and frustration that had begun to overtake me more often as the summer passed, and that was in no way alleviated now by the feel in my pocket of a letter which I had received in the same mail as Laurel's obscene bulletin: sent by my editor in New York, it contained the first review of my book, and although I had not yet read it I could somehow sense that the review was bad.

The Gunner went into a paroxysm of coughing as Dee explained to me: "Daddy's an old-time marine, seen 'em all. Western Front in 1918, Haiti, Nicaragua, Guantánamo—wherever the action was at, Daddy was. Ain't that right, boss man? French girls, Spanish girls, even nigger girls down in Haiti, whenever Daddy went ashore the word got around, 'Stud Jeeter's a-comin', Stud Jeeter of the Horse Marines!' Ain't that right, boss man?"

"Well, Juney," he said, wiping his eyes and with a rattle of phlegm at the back of this throat, "I like to say that I done my time thataway near about as good as the next marine around."

"Tell about that whorehouse in—where was it, Daddy?—

Cuba, wasn't it, you know where they run a movie show on the ceiling and they washes off your pecker with coconut oil. Tell about that."

I was quite frankly unaccustomed to such merry sexual candor between parent and offspring, and I listened restlessly for half an hour or so as the Gunner, coughing and obviously in real distress but still eager to recapture the roustabout joys of other days, methodically anatomized brothels in Havana, Port-au-Prince, and Buenos Aires. But finally the effort seemed too much for him; he half-strangled and turned an ashen gray, and Dee got up and led him out of the room, saying that what his father doubtless needed was a Dr. Pepper at the PX for a pick-me-up.

For a while, after they had gone, I lay on my bed in the terrible heat trying to muster courage to read the review. Having subsequently, over the years, received as much vituperative criticism as any of my colleagues in the trade, and in some respects considerably more, yet having perforce developed an all but impermeable skin, I marvel now as I recall the anguish with which I approached the review—my first as a bona fide writer. It was not, to be sure, a review in the most important sense of the word, being merely a prepublication appraisal in one of the journals of the book-publishing industry. But it must be remembered that it was my initiation. For me it was like a crucible, and I read it with a growing and sickening sense of ruin. I think my editor's "Don't let this bother you" had been the tip-off.

This fat, confident, deafening novel by a young Virginian has received such florid advance raves that it is bound to be widely discussed and widely read even though its author's talent—while by no means inconsiderable—hardly measures up to the extravagant claims being made for it. Set in the country-club atmosphere of a Tidewater Virginia city, the novel chronicles—at sometimes glacial pace—the woes and tribulations of a family which includes a neurotic mother, an alcoholic father, and two daughters—one a cripple and the other a nymphomaniac. Sounds like soap opera? It could be, but isn't, for the twenty-six-year-old author is a skilled wordsmith and has a gift for dialogue and imagery which transforms his witches' brew of guilt, jealousy, and Oedipal longings into a reading experience that often rises excitingly above the book's hackneyed theme. But this newcomer is hardly the literary original he is being hailed as, and too often displays his debt to Faulkner, Warren, McCullers, and even Capote and Speed Lamkin, among other recent recruits to the doom-despair-decay school of southern letters. Nonetheless, despite its shopworn subject matter and all too frequent lapses into "purple" prose, the novel signifies the arrival of an interesting new talent and should be satisfying to those serious readers seeking a change from light hammock reading. (Sept. 10. First printing 10,000.)

—L.K.

I was dead. Dead. Dead as a smelt. Skilled wordsmith. Speed Lamkin. Interesting new talent. Jesus Christ, in debt to Speed Lamkin! In retrospect I can see that the review, snotty as it really might have been, did not comprise the killing hatchet job I was convinced it was as I writhed in agony on that unhappy morning. But I had been cruelly clobbered. I can remember every nuance of my misery and mortification, can—even today—recall each raw detail of my thoughts as they sought to liberate me from this outrage, strove to diminish the intensity of the hurt. "L.K." Who the fuck was "L.K."? Lydia Kerr, surely—some smart-ass twenty-three-year-old Vassar graduate, an English major with a fabricated passion for medieval poetry looking down her snoot at every American novelist since Melville, a parched little dyke with blotched skin living in a Village walk-up filled with *Partisan Review*s, Agatha Christie mysteries, and annotated editions of *Piers Plowman*—but no, a Vassar graduate wouldn't write "wordsmith," or, well, would she? A hater of southerners, then, Leo Kolodny, some failed writer turned hack reviewer, a CCNY type with a heart murmur, piles, and joyless Talmudic eyes, probably teaching a seminar in modern lit at a dismal uptown night school, where he purveyed muddy wisdom about Bellow, Malamud, and the Jewish renaissance. Leo Kolodny *would* use "wordsmith." At any rate, I felt finished as a writer, sick at heart, and that night I went out with Lacy to Jacksonville—the garish honky-tonk town that adjoined the base—and drowned myself in a southern-made beer called Lion, so callow a concoction, and so foul, that the yeast floated in it like minute flakes of snow.

What occurred during the next forty-eight hours was improbable, bizarre, and in certain of its aspects beyond explanation—as it still is to me. When I first started to set down this chronicle, I was tempted not to include the episode (nor for that matter anything at all about Dee Jeeter and his fa-

ther), feeling that it had so little to do with Paul Marriott
that its presence would be superfluous and distracting. But
on second thought I have decided to describe what happened, for I think it tells more about Paul than I had at first
imagined, and about the Marine Corps, and what makes it
such a mysterious community of men.

After coming back from Jacksonville that night I fell into
a drugged sleep, only to be aroused some hours later by a
dreadful racket which was unidentifiable at first and then, as
I came to my senses, resolved itself into the noise of coughing. I sat upright in bed as dawn palely filtered through the
windows. The spasm of coughing—from Gunner Jeeter—
was truly awful to hear, a steady sepulchral hacking so helpless, so rending of the flesh that it seemed to breathe the
very sound of mortality. And to my amazement, when my
eyes accustomed themselves to the dim light, I saw that Dee
had not simply relinquished his bed to his father (my first
thought) but that they were *both* sleeping in it—a bed like
mine, somewhat uncomfortably narrow for one. As I sat listening to the unceasing coughs I was filled with a number of
emotions—chagrin, pity, concern, and, finally, anger. For
while it was bad enough that these characters without so
much as a by-your-leave to me (after all, I outranked both of
them, though not greatly) should for whatever reason (I
ruled out incest) double up in bed and further congest our
tiny sleeping space, it was insufferable that there should be
added to this intrusion such a slumber-destroying uproar.
And why in God's name wasn't the old man in the hospital?

There was a lull in the coughing and I heard Dee say:
"How you feelin', Daddy?"

"Awright," the Gunner replied. "Wisht I had some terrapin hydrate, or some Smith Brothers cherry drops. I'm burnin' up with fever, though. What time is it, son?"

" 'Bout half past five. Why don't you set up, boss man, and have a cigarette? That might soothe you down."

Even in those innocent days before the surgeon general's report, when I myself was a dedicated smoker, I knew that a cigarette was hardly the anodyne for the Gunner's ailment, whatever it might be, and I was about to peevishly say so when he lit his Zippo for a smoke, sitting up weakly in bed, his face a cadaverous white in the glow of the fire. I could not stand the sight. I buried my head in the pillow and slept fitfully until reveille, a cannonade of coughing agitating my dreams like the rumble of a thunder beyond a distant horizon.

When I awoke the pair of them was gone. Later in the day I saw Lacy, who thought the story was howlingly funny but was of the opinion too that in some way, if only for my own health, I should manage to throw the old man out.

"Poor old sod, I feel sorry for him," I said, "but I can't stand another night of that. I just have to get some decent sleep."

"You've *got* to have him evicted," Lacy insisted. "It's not just an imposition on your own rights and privacy, but it sounds to me like he's got a really virulent case of TB. Think of all those bacteria floating down on you. Get him out of there, for Christ's sake!"

That night our company had a compass problem in the woods, and I arrived back at the B.O.Q. after one o'clock, worn out, to face the same ordeal: the drowned sleep, the diabolical interruption, the long hours as I lay, rigid as a mummy, listening to the tormented hacking and hawking and the inane colloquy between father and son. Again only at dawn did I drift off to sleep, awaking a couple of hours later feeling dopey and stupefied, like one who has been given too strong a dose of barbiturates. Both of my room-mates were gone.

I encountered Dee in the shower room a few minutes later. "Where's your father?" I demanded.

"Went down to the mess hall for breakfast," he replied, soaping lather over the acne pits of his jowls. "How's things, old buddy? You surely look bright-eyed and bushy-tailed."

"Then your eyesight is even poorer than you imagined," I said testily. "I've had hardly a moment's sleep in two nights now. Listen, Dee, I want to tell you something. I think your father is in very bad shape physically. I strongly suggest that you get him over to the hospital, and right away. There's something wrong, I mean seriously *wrong*, with a cough like that."

"That's all right. Daddy's always had a lot of trouble with his bronchials, ever since the war of '18. Cough like that just hangs on and hangs on, 'specially after when he gets a cold like he done a week or so ago." Steam from the shaving water had fogged over his glasses and this opaque effect, to-gether with the mounds of white lather, made him seem to me particularly grotesque and repellent. He had just fin-ished stropping an old-fashioned straight-edged razor—a dangerous-looking brilliant thing, the first I had seen in years—and was clothed in only a jockstrap, which I assumed was a necessary accouterment for a knife fighter. "Daddy's goin' to be all right," he went on. "Don't you worry about the ole boss man."

"Well, I don't agree with you," I said, and I heard my

voice grow sharp and impatient. "But even if I did I would still be talking to you this way, because all that coughing is getting in the way of my sleep. I haven't slept for two nights now on account of that coughing. It's as simple as that. I hate to say it, but goddammit, I want your father out of that room today. Do you understand?"

He was silent for a moment, gazing at himself in the mirror, then turned slowly toward me and said in an edgy, evil, smile-when-you-say-that voice: "Gettin' a tiny bit Asiatic, ain't you, ole buddy? What's the matter, tryin' to pull rank on your ole roomie?"

"Just get him out of there," I retorted, feeling an alarming coronary turbulence as I strove to control my rage. "Just get him the fuck out of there, that's all I have to say!" And I turned and left.

Perhaps Dee would finally have complied with my ultimatum; I'll never know. That same day after lunch I returned to the room to change into my dungarees for an afternoon field problem. When I opened the door I immediately sensed something askew, and as I entered the room I saw that the Gunner, alone in the place, propped up feebly at the desk, had begun to hemorrhage; incredibly there was no sound, no coughing now, and very little motion. He merely sat leaning forward slightly with both hands clutched to his mouth, regarding me with a look of silent, abyssal fear. In rivulets the color of freshly decanted claret, blood oozed between his fingers—fingers which seemed fumblingly to be trying to force back between his lips the remorseless flow streaming over the backs of his hands and down his arms. The whole upheaval must have begun only seconds before I arrived. I was riven with panic, having no notion of what to do, whether to lay him down or stand him up, apply manual pressure somewhere or cold compresses, perhaps hot ones, fearful—as one always is when faced with the crisis of first aid—that what one might do would not just be approximately wrong but the exact opposite of right. But I did manage to yell to the corporal, on orderly duty down the hall, to summon an ambulance from the regimental dispensary, and then I grabbed a towel and thrust it into the Gunner's groping hands, figuring that he was better able to soak up the stream than I was. He had begun to moan distantly and his eyes beseeched mine in fathomless terror. And at last I could only stand there helpless, delicately stroking his wasted old shoulders and murmuring foolish words of reassurance while the blood dribbled in vermilion runnels down the stringy arms, across the bruise-hued tattoo of the grand old Marine Corps globe and anchor embossed there God knew how many years ago during some whoring, celebrant shore leave in Seattle or Valparaíso or Shanghai, when those forearms, young and hard as whalebone, belonged to Stud Jeeter of the Horse Marines, and trickling finally into a puddle on the desk amid the candy boxes, the Gene Autry albums, the muscle magazines, the glittering knives. "Juney," I heard him blubber. "I want to see Juney." But I could do nothing about that either.

The ambulance arrived soon, in no more than five minutes, dispatched with that remarkable efficiency of which the military service is rarely but sometimes capable. I accompanied the Gunner to the hospital and stayed there until Dee turned up, all pinched and pale with dread. But there was no hope for his boss man. He had gone into a coma. He died early the next morning, and an autopsy revealed the existence of advanced carcinoma of the lung.

The episode shook me up terribly and left me in a state

of black depression. Why this was so was difficult for me to explain to myself. It hardly involved anything approaching bereavement. My acquaintance with the Gunner, largely nocturnal and unpleasant, had been so brief that I could not say that the gentle quality he had displayed at first encounter had inspired in me even so warm a response as mild liking. And as for a liking for Dee—the squalid fruit of his loins—I had none. Yet obscurely and unshakably I was haunted by the event for days afterward, without success pondering the reason why a man who must have known himself seriously ill had not sought the refuge of a hospital, and feeling a persistent, perhaps unnecessary guilt—he would have died anyway, I kept telling myself—over the fact that I myself had been so dilatory in my efforts to force him to get his lungs attended to.

Several days after all this happened, and Dee had gotten leave to go down to South Carolina to bury his father—having in the meantime, to my great relief, decamped permanently and without explanation from our room, leaving me free and solitary once more—I ran into Paul Marriott at the bar of the officers' club, where he invited me to have a drink. My oversensitiveness at the time still amazes me, but some masochistic impulse had compelled me to carry the review of my book in my wallet, from which I would extract it from time to time and reread it, digesting anew the few patronizing crumbs of praise it contained and at the same moment flagellating myself with its general tone of deprecation. It embarrasses me to recall that I forced it upon Paul to read, which he did, rapidly, with a slight smile.

Saying only, "You don't take that seriously, do you, really?" he handed the review back to me.

"It's a pain in the ass," I groaned, "just an omen of what's to come."

"Bullshit," he replied. "That's the work of someone who's very young or very jealous of you or both, and in any case a mediocrity. Put it out of your mind."

There was such firm, final authority in his reaction and his manner that it gave me tremendous heart, and I drank three martinis in quick succession as a kind of diminutive celebration. Paul, I had noticed before, always drank carefully, even abstemiously, and although at home he had been most generous with alcohol for his guests I noticed that he appeared consciously to hold back, sipping perhaps two very light bourbons with water before dinner and, after the wine, a single brandy and nothing more. In a way this sparing indulgence seemed to suit him, seemed to go with the image he conveyed of a stunning fitness and vitality. He had a superb physique—the kind of supple, feline, coordinated body that one envied so at the age of fourteen, and caused one to send off for a Charles Atlas course in muscle building—and an air of ravishing health: any excess of booze would have soon coarsened and made soggy those remarkably well-proportioned features. Paul was nursing a single bottle of Carlsberg beer. We were joined by a major and a captain, both regulars, whom I was introduced to by Paul, and the talk turned to baseball—a subject which (perversely for an American) tends to bring on in me such devastating ennui that I can feel it as an actual soreness or inflammation at the back of my skull. The conversation here did not descend to anything so ignoble as batting averages; it was Mickey Mantle I think they were talking about, he was very big that year, and they were comparing him to some other batter or pitcher or whatever, from Chicago or Boston or somewhere; I lost track of it all, noting only that Paul spoke knowledgeably and enthusiastically about the sport, which did not seem at all out of character when I recollected that Lacy had told me that he had been a triple-threat athlete at V.M.I. Then after a bit the talk became more general, and I found myself morosely telling about the old Gunner who had started to die in my room just a few days before. Save for Lacy, I had not mentioned the matter to anyone, and now as I described the whole strange event in detail I found that it had for me a liberating, almost cathartic effect.

"I suppose I should have gotten him out of there the first night," I said, "pulled rank on his son or something and made sure that he got some proper treatment. But the doctor at the hospital told me that he was already done for."

"No," said Paul, "you really had no responsibility in the thing. What was the old fellow's name anyway?"

"Jeeter," I said, "regular warrant officer, retired."

Paul's jaw dropped and over his face came a look of sudden dismay. *"No,"* he said, in a slow wondering voice. "No, it's hard to believe—Gunner Jeeter, Stud Jeeter he was called—dead! I can hardly believe it! Fellow with a sort of sad hound dog's face, melancholy eyes?"

"The same," I replied. "Yes."

He shook his head gently and reflectively. "So the Gunner's gone to his reward," he said, and his lips were touched with a wry, mischievous smile. "I only hope there are a lot of hot broads in heaven. The Gunner was one of the greatest swordsmen ever to hit the Corps."

"I've heard of the Gunner, haven't I, Paul?" said one of the other officers. "Wasn't he a Medal of Honor winner in the First World War?"

"No," Paul said. "That decoration he got in Nicaragua during the 1920s, fighting the Communist rebels. Although you are right, he had been with the Fifth Marines at Château-Thierry. Stud Jeeter dead and gone, why it's like the passing of an era!" He sighed and ran his hand through his sandy, close-cropped hair. And an odd expression—remote, searching, reminiscent—came to his eyes, a look that I found unsettlingly brimful of emotion; it was not quite, but manifestly close to, real sorrow, and I discerned a mistiness that for an instant seemed to presage tears. But then he laughed hesitantly and said, "God, he was one of the most colorful characters the Corps has ever seen. Boozer, brawler, whoremonger—and brave as Achilles. Had downed his share of piss and punk, too, but one of the best men with a heavy-machine-gun unit the Corps ever produced. God, I didn't know he had died!" Again the tone was of real chagrin. "I *wish* I'd known! I'll have to go to the funeral."

"I believe the funeral was yesterday," I put in, "down in South Carolina."

"Did you know the Gunner, Paul?" one of the officers inquired. The captain and the major, though older than myself by a few years, were considerably younger than Paul, and when they asked these questions about the Gunner, all eager and attentive, I was reminded of something almost tribal—of junior Apache or Sioux braves in the presence of a wiser, more seasoned chieftain, seeking a word of a fabled place and time, of heroes who fought before the reservations existed, when the buffalo thronged the plains and drums beat along the warpath. The Old Corps.

"He was truly one of the Old Breed," Paul mused. "They don't make them like that anymore. Hell, yes, I knew him, I knew the Gunner well. My first year of sea duty as a lieutenant, on the *Maryland,* he was a sergeant in the marine detachment. That was in '32 or '33, and he taught me everything about sea duty I ever knew. Then later on, when I was in Shanghai before the war, the Gunner was there—a warrant officer by then—and again he taught me as much about infantry tactics as I ever learned at Quantico. He was too old to get in the fighting in the last war, and not in very good health, either. The liquor eventually got at him. I think he finally developed a diabetes that put him out of commission. He never would see a doctor, even in Shanghai when he was having terrible trouble with his liver. So I don't wonder that just now he wouldn't go to the hospital, even when he was coughing his guts up. Son of a bitch! What a *sorry,* pathetic way for the old fellow to go out! I'm sad that I didn't know he was up here, that I somehow couldn't have paid a last goodbye."

Appropriately, as Paul spoke (indeed, with an appropriateness that could only be called banal), the sound of a bugle fell on the late-afternoon air and I glanced outside the club where a flag was being lowered while the bugler blew "Retreat," and a scattering of marines had paused at momentary attention, their figures casting lean, gangly shadows in the slant of sunset. And for a long instant I was seized— as I always have been when I hear those piercing trumpet notes—with a sense of loss and sadness, a vision of tropic seas and strange coasts, storm-swept distances accompanied always and always in my mind's innermost recess with the muffled tramp of booted footfalls, as of legions of men being hurried to unknown destinies. Then the sound of the bugle died away and I heard Paul's voice again through the growing clatter of the bar, where the officers' wives' unbridled laughter and "My Truly, Truly Fair," booming from the Muzak, battled each other over the incessant churning of the cocktail shakers.

"And so his boy became a marine, did he?" he said to me. "He was so proud of that kid. The last time I saw the Gunner—it must have been ten years ago, in San Diego, just after Pearl Harbor—he said he only wished his boy had been born early enough to fight in the war. But he also said no matter, his kid would be a marine someday. And so he is. How he adored that boy! He'll get his chance in Korea. Nice fellow?"

"Charming," I said, misty-eyed.

"That Gunner!" Paul exclaimed. "Christ, you know he wouldn't salute any officer less than flag grade, and there were even some colonels he wouldn't give the time of day to. Wore his dungarees everywhere, even at parade. What a character!" He went on with a smile, shaking his head, deeply moved, reminiscent: "You know, in 1942 they had surveyed him out for medical reasons at Pendleton—he must have been over fifty then—yet they couldn't make him quit. Here he was, technically separated from the service, and he had the gumption, the grit—the *brass* to hitch a ride, I mean literally stow away on a transport going to Pearl Harbor, where he stormed into the commanding general's office—in his dungarees, mind you—and demanded that he be assigned to duty somewhere in the First Division. He meant Guadalcanal, too, and no rotten office job. Of course, he couldn't make it, but what *grit*, what splendid *brass*! No sir, they don't make marines like the Gunner anymore. Did you ever hear how he won that Medal of Honor—"

The Old Corps. Suddenly I understood that despite

Paul's vivid anecdotal style I really didn't give a damn how the old fart had gotten his Medal of Honor—and this was truly still a measure of my disaffection with the Corps and all it stood for. Paul, however, had warmed to his subject with all the vivacity and zeal of one of those pukka sahib types, usually played by David Niven, memorializing vanished exploits on the Afghan border; and just as my disappointment in Paul became sharpest and most vexing I realized how foolish it was for me to feel that way: he was a marine above all, first and foremost, *always* a marine, and for me it had been the dreamiest wishful thinking, goofy as a schoolgirl's, to see him as truly "literary" or "artistic" when these were merely components of an enlightened and superior dilettantism. It was extraordinary enough that those delicate aspects of his personality had not been obliterated by the all-demanding, all-molding pressures of the military system, had not been trampled by the ruthless boot of an organization insisting of its members that their sensibilities remain male and muscular, their culture sterile, ingrown, and philistine if not mindless. He had read Camus. This alone, it seemed to me, was almost a miracle.

The bugle call still lingered in my mind, suffusing me with a mood both restless and somber, and as I sat there in the twilight listening to Paul's stories about the Gunner, listening to his warm and feeling panegyric to this old departed mercenary warrior, to these tales of the Old Corps with their memories and echoes of sea duty and shore leave, of jungle bivouacs, of Haitian outposts, Nicaraguan patrols, Chinese skirmishes, and other relics of America's magisterial thrusts and forays throughout the hemisphere and the world, I realized that Paul was certainly at least as comfortable, if not more so, when talking of these matters as about French cuisine or the gentle art of fiction. He was a professional, and the ties to the small elite fellowship to which he belonged—ties of nostalgia as well as loyalty and faith—were as strong (and no more to be wondered at) in the end as those ties which bind other men to a vocation in science or the arts or a political belief or—to be more nearly precise—a church.

THE SUICIDE RUN

I MUST MAKE A SMALL CONFESSION. Despite my aversion to military things, there are aspects of the life that I have found tolerable—fascinating even, though inferior to chess or Scarlatti. Take mortars, for example. Although I was born with, I'm sure, less than average manual dexterity, the use of mortars in the field—and my ability to supervise the men who handled them—never failed to please me in its neat meshing of teamwork, speed, subtlety of reflex, and mechanical skill. Rather like an athletic ballet with men in almost synchronous motion, the whole process of setting up the long tubes on their bipods and baseplates, locating the aiming stakes, precisely leveling and balancing the weapons with their various little cranks and wheels—all of these comprised a nimble, exciting prelude to the penultimate racket as the rounds popped forth on their lethal journey through the empyrean and to the final, gratifying, earth-jolting *crump-crump* when—a mile away—the shells blew some poor nigger shack to sawdust. To be sure, it was never so neat and pretty in combat. Nevertheless, I think it all satisfied a thwarted boyish longing in me, a desire for the loudest and fattest firecracker in the world, though in addition there was something unnervingly priapean about those stiff uptilted tubes poking the air, and my pleasure may have been rooted in a darker source; whatever, the sense of rhythm, precision, and completion I achieved from working with mortars helps provide another reason why military service and infantry combat in particular is such a magic lure for certain men.

Of course it was not unheard of, during training, for a mortar to burst apart with dreadful effect, killing or maiming everyone nearby, and once that summer—in another regiment—several faulty rounds fell disastrously short of the target and blotted out the lives of eight young recruits; such eventualities occasionally caused me to sweat and made my mouth grow dry with fear. But in general I managed to avoid thoughts like these and took pleasure in the work. In fact, rather paradoxically, it was the severely military aspects of my recall to service which I liked the most, or minded the least. My flesh had fallen into soft disrepair in the stews of Greenwich Village; the new routine was strenuous, with many days and nights on training problems, amphibious landings, and sadistic hikes, and after the first shock wore off it was an actual delight to develop a trooper's appetite and to feel the muscle tone return to my flabby, once-sodden limbs.

I acquired a glorious suntan: a couple of snapshots taken of me at the time record the very figure of a strapping, bronzed, miserable young marine. But I had forgotten how appealing, how spirit-enhancing sheer physical exertion could be, and as I galloped through the swamps and woods with my merry crew of mortarmen I was curiously relieved of my bitter discontent—as if in a perverse way the closer my proximity was to the grime and sweat of the battle, and the more intent became my preoccupation with the niceties of infantry tactics, the less I was harried by that pitiless anxiety.

No, what brought me closest to true despair was not the war games or even the frequent lectures on subjects like field sanitation, cargo loading, and the Communist menace (I could usually sleep through these), but the periods of leisure—in the evenings or on weekends—when the free time I had allowed me to reflect on the awfulness of my future. To gripe bitterly in the company of my fellow sufferers provided some solace, but its cathartic effect was ultimately limited. Therefore, during my off-duty hours at the base I retreated more and more into a private world, seeing my friend Lacy now and then or, locked in my sweltering room, poring over the galley proofs of my first novel with all the finicky vigilance of a medieval scholastic and, finally, indulging myself in epic sessions of both fancy and plain onanism. I am sure that it was during this summer at Lejeune that I shed once and for all whatever guilt I had ever possessed about the unnameable sin, Christendom's vilest. Having deprived me of an outlet for my needs, the Marine Corps could at least not outwit me when it came to my innermost dreams, and I embarked on a one-man orgy that in slyness and ingenuity would have outstripped the fancy of Alexander Portnoy. Certainly enforced sexual famine is one of the most important keys to an understanding of the genius of the military mystique: cause a soldier to ache with such longing for the odor of a woman's flesh that it becomes an insupportable rage, and you have often created a man who will grab a bayonet and coolly eviscerate Aggressor Enemy.

To put it simply, I thought the chances were extremely good that I would die without ever getting laid again, and much of my extra-military energy was spent trying to prevent this from happening—even though it occurs to me now that my frantic pursuit of the goal brought me once very close to sudden death. And so a word about this—

I was by then receiving letters almost daily from my "mistress," I suppose you could call her, Laurel—feverish, highly spiced messages in a blatantly legible hand acquired at Miss Hewitt's. I understand that it is rare for a lady to develop a full-blown pornographic style, but my darling's imagination was stunningly lewd; the raunchy letters, often written on her husband's stationery—"F. Edward Lieberman, M.D. Practice Limited to Ear, Nose and Throat"— though they made me only to a small degree sorry for old Ed, had an effect on my glands which ever afterward rendered insipid the word "aphrodisiac." Our present era of air travel had only commenced then, and New York was still more than five hundred miles away by unimproved highway and train; through superhuman exertion, however, it was barely possible (on those infrequent weekends when circumstances caused us to be at liberty as early as the middle of Saturday afternoon) to drive at suicidal speeds the three hundred miles to Washington, where one could board a train that arrived in Manhattan just before the bars closed at three on Sunday morning. It was a ridiculously abbreviated visit—one had to leave New York no later than nine the next evening in order to be back at the base by reveille on Monday morning—and the lack of sleep it entailed still awes me. But such was our desperation to escape the nightmare in which we found ourselves—and so tormenting was my crucifixion of lust—that Lacy and I made the insane journey every time the chance presented itself.

And so, already exhausted from days and nights in the swamps, we would barrel out of camp in Lacy's Citroën, heading north at terrible speed. Even so, the French had not built that model to go as fast as we might have wished. In compensation, Lacy was a sharp-witted, aggressive driver with reflexes that seemed almost computerized, so swiftly and correctly did they discriminate between the long chance and indubitably fatal error; my heart capered wildly when on one of those two-lane Carolina roads at seventy miles an hour—against opposing traffic—he overtook some huge lumber truck, throwing the car into its next-to-last gear just in time to edge in ahead and with so little margin to spare that I felt more than once the oncoming truck or car trade with us a great soughing whoosh, as the Citroën quivered with the strain. Yet each time I realized how exquisitely Lacy had maneuvered—the entire job far more a display of coolness and timing than of any machismo. Sometimes I took turns driving with Lacy. I was not anywhere near as skillful as he was, and far less nervy, but even so I performed stunts that can make me feel queasy when I think of them to this day: a race to an unbarricaded grade crossing with an Atlantic Coast Line passenger train, for instance, when I gunned past the blinking red warning lights at such speed that the car, mounting the crowned hump of the tracks, literally sailed through the air like some resurrected image from the Keystone Kops and regained the asphalt on the other side only seconds before the engine pounded past us, trumpeting in a frenzy. For a long time afterward, I recall, Lacy and I sat in feeble silence while the dusty emerald tobacco fields swept by, and the forlorn stretches of marshland and pine slumbered in the heat, until at last Lacy, shaken but in grasp of the lovely aplomb I had grown accustomed to in him, said in a distant voice: "Twenty-four kilometers to Saint-Jean-de-Luz. Do you like *moules marinières?*"

But the time I truly saw the face of death was not then— it was worse even than this wrenching scare—and it is important to me not alone for the aspect it presented, memorable yet somehow ultimately banal, but for the strange vision the same encounter evoked in Lacy, a vision which he told me about and which I've never forgotten.

We had arrived at Penn Station at some hour in the dark of Sunday morning—encrusted with the dust of twenty North Carolina and Virginia counties and the grime of the Pennsylvania Railroad's most senile and airless parlor car— and had debarked into the arms of our eager girls. Their very presence was like a renewal of life: Lacy's wife, Annie, very French-looking, not really beautiful but possessing oval provocative eyes and a luminous smile, and, beside her, Laurel, not really beautiful either but with tousled blond hair and adorable lips parted in moist, concupiscent welcome. They bore no gifts but themselves, which was more than enough.

There followed then the usual scenario (this being not an exact rendition of that particular visit but—alas, for my poor memory—a synthesis of those several times): after a quick good-bye to Lacy and Annie I hurry with Laurel to the taxi ramp, where she has foresightedly kept a cab waiting.

We have spoken to each other a few words—cheerful, oblig-
atory, with a slight tremolo betraying our madness: "Hello,
honey. Gee, you look good. How was the trip?" She crawls
into the cab with the modesty of a stripper, exposing the
inner slope of a thigh tanned at Fire Island and—through
the interstices of black peekaboo panties—rosy hints of her
marvelously supple, inverted-heart-shaped ass. Suddenly I
realize that I am running a fever—no mere hectic lovesick
flush, either, but the high fever of terminal illness, pneumo-
nia, anthrax, plague. I sink next to her, surround her with my
arms, and hear myself utter a demented gargling sound as
the cab heads south toward the Village. Along Ninth Avenue
oblongs of neon, green and red, flash through my clenched
eyelids, and the wet interplay of our tongues astounds me.
Slick tongues, darkly wrestling, underwater shapes, they
dominate all my sensations—save for the feel of her indus-
trious fingers at work on my fly, with its critical tumescence,
and with its stuck zipper. And that is just as well, I am able
to reflect even then; satisfied that no precipitate "petting to
climax"—in the sexologist's odious phrase—might vitiate
any of the mortal lovemaking left to me.

And so together, in a borrowed basement apartment on
Christopher Street—and it is necessary neither to describe
the rococo fictions Laurel employs in order to spend a night
away from Dr. Lieberman and Fire Island on a beautiful
summer weekend, nor to dwell in any great detail upon the
amatory rites performed in our incandescent little hideaway.
That Laurel is a thoroughgoing adept in bed has already
been made clear. She also commands a huskily vocal, horta-
tory, descriptive style that I find compatible with my own in-
clination—though I certainly need no inducement to boost

a flagging appetite. But right now (and the apparatus of boudoir photography comes to mind), despite my suspicion that to employ the zoom lens would be a technique falling somewhere between the mandatory and the trendy, I must draw back, out of the feeling that such efforts will produce only another stale portrait of fornication, irrelevant and distracting. No, what stands out most clearly from this distant vantage point is not a glimpse of the tanned, entangled bas-relief of our screwing (like me, she occasionally enjoys mirrors, or professes to) but the sheer urgency, the almost amnesiac concentration I place in the service of my passion—as if by subsuming my entire self to an awareness of my groin I might obliterate the future, validate life, and triumph over the terror of extinction. Sleep is in abeyance, too time-devouring to be indulged in; we seem never to be unjoined; the light of dawn seeps through the window, midmorning arrives, then noon. At three in the afternoon we are still at it, awash, bruised, scratched, aching, and only then do I doze for a few minutes, awaking to find her in tears as she crouches above me. "You *men*," she weeps, "all the good *fucking* there is to be had in the world and you men blow it all to hell by going to *war*! There must be something *wrong* with you men!" And then I have one long, luscious, ferocious go at her, reaching oblivion a final time before, irrevocably, it is the moment to leave—to shower and sleepily dress, to have a lingering, gluttonous, late Sunday afternoon meal in a good Italian restaurant on Bleecker Street, and at last to meet Lacy at Penn Station just before eight o'clock. . . . End of scenario. Total time elapsed: seventeen hours.

But somehow it was all too much, too brutal, frantic, and there came a point when I realized that the word "suicidal"—by which even then I characterized these journeys—was not at all facetious and that in the starkest way there was contained in these desperate weekends the powerful essence of self-destruction. Returning in the car to the base on Monday morning at dawn, after a New York visit that had been especially exhausting, mainly because of this marathon venery but also because of a train that was two hours behind schedule, and because of the train itself with its heat and its sordid flatulence, its bellowing candy butchers and its relentless onslaught of shrieks from tormented babies, and because of the desolating effect of newspaper headlines announcing huge marine casualties in Korea, and because of a flat tire we had to change outside of Richmond, in pouring rain—returning this morning with a sore throat and the runny beginnings of a summer cold, I had the feeling (and I sensed Lacy's sharing it) that rather than endure another such pilgrimage I would willingly allow myself to be sent to combat and let the Chinese get a hunk of my pelt or my balls, or even my life. I was so tired that my bones ached, forestalling real sleep, and as I half-drowsed I had become the prey of crazy hot flashes and prickly little hallucinations. I had driven the first long lap from Washington down to Emporia, Virginia, while Lacy tried to sleep; now Lacy had been driving for several hours across the Carolina tidewater, murderously forcing the Citroën to its uttermost limit as we plowed through the twilit pearly light of dawn, swirling with patches of dusty fog that breathed up out of level monotonous fields of tobacco and green cotton.

I recall vividly that I was dreaming of a raffish assembly of gnomes, garbed as in drawings from the tales by the brothers Grimm, who were holding a *Bierfest* in an autumn garden. They gesticulated toward me and called to me in involute German, a language of which I knew about twenty words. Fluently, I called back to them and waved a greeting, while in the midst of this delirium my eyes snapped open to behold, or sense, or somehow apprehend simultaneously, two horrors: Lacy, nodding, eyes partly shut, hands deathly limp, half asleep at the wheel—and a huge trailer truck dead ahead, nosing out into our path. I do not know—I'll never know—how close we were to the truck, to that intersection on the outskirts of some little farming town where the red stoplight winked at us mindlessly and serenely through the mists. I do know we were so near to collision that certain details are still as clear as those startling protuberances in a trompe l'oeil painting—the truck itself, hauling bags of fertilizer, browsing through the fog like a mastodon; the Negro driver's bare blue-black shiny elbow perched on the window ledge and the alarmed eyes of the Negro like eggshells, rolling toward us; the great red sign on the truck, VIRGINIA-CAROLINA CHEMICAL: all of these shards of recognition were for half a second separate, random, before at once becoming merged into a single terrifying image of annihilation.

"Oh shit, Lacy!" I yelled. And at that he came awake and alive, and began a herculean effort to ransom us from the grave. I still do not know how he did it; his hand spun the wheel, his foot hit the brake, and we veered awfully. I heard him gasp, heard too the scream of the tires, locked now, and my own voice repeating, "*Shit*, Lacy! Shit, shit, shit, oh *shit!*" as we lurched and yawed from side to side and skidded straight toward the trailer's murderously glinting undercarriage, waiting to shred us into junk and bloody pulp. On and on we hurtled, squealing. I saw the Negro's elbow go up in a wild disjointed motion and at that instant a burst of blue exhaust smoke plumed aloft from the truck's cab. It may be that this meant that the driver's own foot slammed down on the gas, that his own scared reflex provided the margin for the salvation of all, his included; whatever it was that saved us—his panic or Lacy's cunning at the wheel or both, or the providence that attends innocent black truck drivers and marines fatigued to the brink of death—we squeaked through, missing the rear end of the trailer by what was clearly bare inches, and sideslipped to a jolting, vibrating halt in a weed-choked ditch. Although for long moments we were voiceless with fright, neither of us was even bruised, and the spunky Citroën had received not a nick or dent.

"Is you all right?" I heard the Negro's voice call from up the road where he had stopped his rig.

Lacy flapped his hand in limp reassurance and after a pause shouted, "Sorry, man!" in a hoarse, broken voice. Then he put his head down against the steering wheel. I heard a muffled giggle, and what appeared to be shudders of hysteric relief coursed through his shoulders. Finally without another word he sat erect and started the car, and we proceeded again through the dawn, moving at a dignified old lady's pace.

After several miles I managed to find words to speak, something banal and hollow like the ugly little episode itself. I cast a sidelong glance at Lacy, who for a long while had said nothing. The sensitively drawn, almost pretty face in profile had suddenly taken on a pinched and bitter cast: through the unblemished tan the boyish features were not really boyish but haggard, aging. When at last he spoke it was in a grave tone edged with anguish, and it was filled with marked, unsettling intensity, as if our dangerous escape had unloosened in him some fear long held in precarious restraint.

"I saw that motherfucking dog again," he said.

"What dog?" I said. "*Again?*" For an instant I thought he might have been made temporarily addled. "Where?"

He drove on for a while without speaking. Then he said, "See that?" and held up his right hand. There small shiny mounds of scar tissue, perhaps five or six of them, traversed the palm in a ragged crescent. I had seen these marks before. Assuming they were scars from a combat wound, obviously not now incapacitating, I had never bothered to ask him how they had come about, nor had Lacy ever volunteered an explanation—until now.

"It was toward the end of the fighting on Okinawa in '45," he said. "I had a rifle platoon in the Sixth Marines. It was in June, I remember, around noon on a June day and hotter—as an old gunny friend used to say—than the downtown part of hell. Our battalion had been on the assault for two days, trying to wipe out a dinky little town where the Japs had set up an especially strong position. They had artillery in there, a lot of heavy stuff, lot of mortars, and we'd been taking a terrible pounding. But we managed to break them down pretty well with our own big guns and several air strikes, and my company moved up, as I say, around noon, to mop up along a couple of the streets of the town."

He paused and I saw him reflectively rub his scarred palm along the edge of his cheekbone. "Well, just as we moved out of the fields toward the edge of the village we began to get clobbered from a Jap mortar position which had somehow missed getting finished off by our guns. They were suicidal little bastards, you know—this was also along about the time of the kamikaze attacks—and they were determined to take us with them; that's why it was such miserable fighting. Anyway, we hit the deck at the edge of the road, I slid into a shallow little ditch full of muck, and that mortar began to pound the shit out of us. It was as dirty a barrage as I'll ever want to go through. They were zeroed in on us, firing for effect, and why or how I didn't get hit I'll never know. It must have gone on for a full five minutes or more when suddenly I looked up from where I was lying and saw, on the other side of the road, directly opposite and no more than four or five yards away, a big black skinny dog, standing there with his four legs sort of akimbo, simply out of his mind with fear at this bombardment going on around him.

"I must have made some sort of motion with my body then, raising up slightly. Although of course I fire from my right shoulder, I'm left-handed and was holding my carbine in my left hand, trying to keep it out of the muck. As I raised up then, the dog just *flew* at me from the road, and before I knew it he had his jaws clamped down and completely through the palm of my free hand. It was utterly insane, a nightmare, you see—this mortar barrage, with guys getting chopped up all around me, and here this wild terrified dog had sunk his fangs into my hand, so tight that I could not make him let go, as much as I struggled and yanked and pulled. The dog didn't make any noise, didn't growl, didn't snarl, simply glared at me with these mad wet eyes and chomped away at my hand. The pain was—well, beyond description; I don't recall whether I screamed or not. My platoon sergeant was not far away but even if he had seen all this he couldn't have done anything, pinned down like all the rest. Ah Jesus, every time I think of it my hand begins to ache all over again."

"What in God's name did you do finally?" I asked.

"I knew I had to shoot the dog, but it's damned hard to fire a carbine, you know, or at least aim it well with one hand, and besides for some dumb reason I had the weapon on safety. Yet I knew I had to shoot him. And God knows I was trying to. And I kept looking at that goddam dog, kept looking into those crazy eyes. There was something—something, well, retributive, demonic about those eyes. How can I say it? It was as if for a moment I felt I was getting in a curious way my just deserts—that this dog represented all those innocent victims who are crazed and mutilated by war and finally have to lash out at their tormentors, seizing upon the first poor uniformed slob that comes to hand. A fantasy, of course—the poor beast was simply berserk with terror— but that's what did flash through my mind."

"And of course you finally got him?" I said.

"Yeah," he went on, "I finally got that carbine around, and somehow worked it off safety, and shot him through the head. It was sickening, ghastly. And after the Jap mortars slackened off and the company could move ahead it took the corpsman at least five minutes to pry that dog's fangs out of my hand. And that was the end of the war for me, because that same afternoon I was evacuated to the rear and sent out to a hospital ship for precautionary anti-rabies treatment. It was while I was getting this long course of shots—a bloody painful business, I might add—that the campaign ended on Okinawa."

He fell silent for a moment. We were not far now from the camp, and the early-morning traffic had begun to fill the roads—farmers in pickup trucks, tourists with Florida license plates heading north for the summer, marines commuting to work at the base. Lacy drove very slowly, and with extreme care.

"Ah God," he said at last, in a somber, grieving tone. "We'll *never* make it through *this* war."

MY FATHER'S
HOUSE

ONE MORNING IN THE YEAR AFTER the end of the war (the Good War, that is, the second War to End All Wars) when I had returned to my father's house in Virginia, and had slept long merciful hours, I woke up after completing a weird megalomaniacal dream. Not that I was unaccustomed to dreams touched with megalomania. A few years before, for example, when I was a writing student at college, I had a dream about James Joyce. In this particular reverie I was sitting at a café table somewhere in Europe, probably Paris, having a cup of coffee with the Master. There was no hesitancy in the way he turned his purblind gaze upon me, no embarrassment in the sudden light touch of his hand on the back of my own, nor was there anything but nearly mawkish admiration in his Hibernian brogue as he uttered these words: "Paul Whitehurst, your writing has been such an inspiration to me! Without your work I could not have finished *Dubliners*!"

I never thought I'd recapture the mad glee that seized me upon waking from such a cockeyed fantasy. And during the war I had no similar visitations. But the end of that exhausting conflict brought me such relief that I suppose it was inevitable that another such dream should return, rescuing my near-drowned ego. In this sequence I was seated next to Harry Truman as we cruised in a limousine down Pennsylvania Avenue. "Paul Whitehurst"—once again the full name, precisely enunciated—"the best advice you ever gave me was to drop the atom bomb." Amid pennants snapping in the wind and the blare of military music, I nodded left and right to the adoring throng. "Thank you, Mr. President," I replied. "I gave it much thought."

And waking, I lay there for a while, helplessly disgorging cackles of laughter. At last the dream faded away, as dreams do. Then I made my mind a blank. Finally, the sound of breakfast being made was borne upstairs and I inhaled the good smell and prepared for the new day.

Except for a central drawback, which I'll soon deal with, I was fairly contented in my father's house. The house itself inspired a kind of contentment. My father had never been a rich man, but the war with its naval contracts had brought prosperity to the sprawling shipyard where he toiled nearly all of his life; his share in the prosperity had allowed him to move from the cramped little bungalow of my childhood to an unpretentious, comfortable, locust-shaded house whose screened porch and generous bay windows faced out on a grand harbor panorama. The enormous waterway, several miles across, was always afloat with an armada of naval ships or seabound tankers and freighters—all distant enough to be dramatic-looking rather than unsightly—and the harbor was forever being touted by the local boosters as the rival or the superior of San Francisco or Rio or Hong Kong, though to my mind they were exaggerating badly since the panorama was really too monotonous, too horizontal, to be "breathtakingly scenic," as was claimed.

Nonetheless, it was impressive in its way. Certainly I would concede that my father had bought himself a million-dollar view—he called it that at nearly every opportunity—and so I considered the fine expanse of water, sparkling in the sun or swept by rude squalls or echoing at night with mournful horns, to be one of the more amiable bonuses of my homecoming from the war. Tidewater summers were fiercely hot and dank but the harbor often bestowed on the house an early cooling breeze—"a million-dollar breeze," my father would say on the more hellish days. I'd awake beneath the sheet and stretch while the odor of coffee and pancakes filled my nose, and then I'd smile. What I mean is that I was conscious of making a genuine, broad, cheek-dimpling smile while I marveled over and over at my healthy living state, in which the primitive ability to smell warm pancakes and coffee was like a surprising gift. There is no mystery why these first waking moments were so luxuriously free of anxiety, why a shiver of pleasure—no, real *bliss*—ran through me when I blinked awake on the sun-splashed bed, listening to the mockingbird in the locust outside my window or, farther off, the gulls and shorebirds piping over the water, a Negro flower peddler, a horse cart creaking (there were still a few horses and carts in those days, though fast vanishing), clip-clopping hooves, the cry of "Flowers, flowers!" skewering my heart as it had done when I was a child. My happiness, my bliss, was quite simple in origin: I was *alive*. I was alive and home in bed instead of being a moving target on the Kyushu plain, or in the rubble of an Osaka suburb, praying for one more day of life in the cauldron of a war without ending— what a miracle, what a gift! So many times, only months before, death had seemed such a certainty that my very *aliveness* became a recurrent marvel.

It was hard, however, to avoid a shiver of guilt when I reflected on my luck. Over three years before, when I was seventeen, bravado mingled with what must have been a death wish made me enlist in the officer training program of the Marine Corps. Since those in my age group were considerably too callow to lead troops into battle, it was decided at the Navy Department that we be sent to college, where as book-toting privates we would gain a little learning and seasoning, also a year or two of physical and mental growth, before our fateful collision with the Japs. My classmates and I, being the youngest of the young, remained uniformed college students for the longest period, while those who were only a year or so older went off for the officer training and preceded us into those terrifying island battles that marked the last stages of the Pacific war. No group among all the services had so high a casualty rate as we Marine Corps second lieutenants. This is firmly on the record. A harrowing book by an enlisted combat veteran, E. B. Sledge, called *With the Old Breed,* described the situation concisely: "During the course of the long fighting on Okinawa . . . we got numerous replacement lieutenants. They were wounded or killed with such regularity that we rarely knew anything about them . . . and saw them on their feet only once or twice. . . . Our officers got hit so soon and so often that it seemed to me the position of second lieutenant in a rifle company had been made obsolete by modern warfare."

Thus had I been older only by a year or so I would have been immersed in Iwo Jima's bloodbath; a mere six months and I would have been one of Sledge's Okinawa martyrs, obliterated in what turned out to be the deadliest land engagement of the Pacific war, and among the worst in history. I actually escaped this horror by a hair, coming to roost not so many miles away on the island of Saipan, where I began to prepare for the invasion of Japan and where I had ample time to reflect on both what I'd barely missed on Okinawa and Iwo Jima and what I was likely to encounter when I helped storm the fortress beaches of the mainland. The killing grounds of the recent past were for me merely a foretaste of things to come, and the sorry fate of all those scared but uncomplaining guys we'd said good-bye to seemed to foreshadow my own.

At any rate, there in bed I'd begin to grope and caress myself, getting a huge load of tactile satisfaction from the mere act of assessing my body's well-being. This was not the idle feeling up of one's self that preoccupies people alone in bed; it was a deliberate, meditative inventory of my precious parts. Consider hands and fingers alone, for example, and place them in the context of the Iwo Jima I so narrowly escaped. Everyone had heard about the landing beach at Iwo: bodies cut in half in the volcanic dust, legs and arms from a single corpse separated by forty feet, a purée of brains splattered among the mess kits and knapsacks. Nearly every marine who survived the war had fixed in his mind the number of Iwo Jima casualties—twenty-six thousand (of which nearly six thousand were deaths)—the entire population of many an American large town or small city, a chilling total of which thousands of components had to be hands and fingers, given the tendency of the hand, with its constant diligence and exposure, to be so vulnerable. Pondering the tally of fingers lost or mutilated on that infernal ash heap, I'd concentrate on one of my own, extend it, wiggle it, stroke it with my thumb, suck it, rub its tip gently against the skin encasing my rib cage, all the while reflecting on what pleasure it was to be able to perform any one of these small, innocuous, monkey-like operations.

Another matter was the loss of limbs. Leg loss and arm loss had been epidemic in the Pacific. What a delight it was, then, to be able to palpate the supple buttery flesh of the biceps, pressing in so deeply with the thumb that I could feel the sturdy arterial flow of healthy blood as it coursed down the arm, or to vigorously pat the muscles of the thigh—the joy momentarily fading, replaced by a stab of guilt as I wondered what it must be like, at that very instant, to be lying without a thigh in some naval hospital, racked by the phantom pain of the amputee.

You could lose incredible parts of yourself, and be hideously mutilated, yet still live. In college I had known this guy named Wade Hoopes, from a small town in Tennessee, who was also a platoon leader at the time of his calamity. He and his little group had been reconnoitering the outskirts of a shell-shattered village on Okinawa when he stepped on a booby-trapped grenade and instantaneously lost a leg. Only the miraculous ministrations of a medical corpsman saved him from bleeding to death. He had wanted to get a law degree when the war ended and make it big in Tennessee politics like his daddy, a onetime lieutenant governor. Wade was generous and sweet-natured, with an incipient politician's chatty bonhomie; I don't think he was brilliant, but that too fitted the political mold. One thing I recall achingly about

Wade Hoopes was the idiot crush he had on June Allyson, and the album of publicity photographs of her that he carried around everywhere—probably even to Okinawa—of June in swimsuits and bobby sox and dirndls, smiling her enchantingly bucktoothed, germ-free smile. It was amazing to think of him whacking off day in and day out over this squeaky-clean sweetheart. A blade of shrapnel from the same booby trap that removed his leg had neatly destroyed his brain's speech center and he would never utter a word again—not a word, not a sound, not a peep. Literally struck dumb. When news came back to our training base on Saipan about Wade Hoopes we were shocked, and our speculation was that when the war was over an amputee might easily make it as a candidate—the sympathy vote. But a politician without a voice? It was like a beauty queen without tits. Otherwise his vital signs were excellent, which may or may not have been a blessing. But we all thought: At least he made it.

I listened to my stepmother, Isabel, clattering and banging away down below in the kitchen while my father, in the nearby bathroom, performed his operatic ablutions. He had a creditable tenor voice, a little reedy but resolute, and as he went about his bathroom business he warbled snatches of Verdi and Puccini and Mozart operas that he'd picked up from old Caruso recordings and the Saturday afternoon Metropolitan broadcasts on the radio. These he tried to duplicate in wildly mispronounced phonetic Italian. The language is not meant to be sung by Anglo-Saxons. It took me a long time to realize that the words I heard above the flushing toilet or blurted halfway through a gargle were *Dalla sua pace* and *Il mio tesoro*. More often what I heard was invented Italian, fruity vocables such as *lalalala—Dio!* or *lalalala—amore!* I regularly had breakfast with my father before we went our separate ways, I to school and he to the shipyard in an automobile full of his white-collar brethren, known as cost estimators, who were members of a car pool.

All this was long before the death of my mother and before he met Isabel, a lady who had become a small but piercing nail thrust into my psyche. I listened to her kitchen commotion. Isabel was a good cook and her talents extended well beyond putting together an appetizing breakfast—there was no way I could begrudge her that. It was one of her contradictions, really, since it was hard for me to accept the idea that this straitlaced, pleasure-shunning person, a professional nurse with a palate anesthetized by hospital food and the chicken croquettes served at the Bide-A-Wee Tearoom, where she and her fellow spinster nurses dined in the years before she snagged my father, could prepare not merely an edible but a, by God, truly flavorsome meal. I suspect it was due to my father's influence. While scarcely a gourmet he had been reared on traditional southern cooking, which at its best is delectable; despite the fact that she had him pretty well under her thumb he had made it clear, I think, that he expected her to set a good table and she had risen to the challenge. So I had to chalk one up for Isabel. Her labors downstairs at breakfast—at least considered from my vantage point in bed, before we came face to face—always left me better disposed toward her than at any other time of the day. Even though she made a lot of noise. She was an ungainly woman, angular and raw-boned, and she tramped about the kitchen with a kind of hulking agitation; I wondered how she had succeeded at her nursing chores, which I conceived as requiring a low-keyed gentleness, an adagio grace beyond this woman's capacity.

Lying there, I occasionally reflected with a chill upon what might have happened to me had my father married her, say, five years earlier than he did, when I was a child of ten or so; she would have gobbled me up. As it was, I was fifteen when they tied the knot, and so I was able to avoid any real damage she might have inflicted, chiefly because school and college claimed me, and then the marines. So I wasn't at home all that often. I racked my head in an attempt to figure out the cause of our mutual hostility, but came up with nothing. From the beginning I was not so naïve as to be unaware of the wicked stepmother myth. A stepmother was *supposed* to be a termagant, a ball-breaker. Lucky was the boy or girl (especially an only child like me) who drew a sweet and loving stepmother; they were *supposed* to be ungenerous, jealous, spiteful, suspicious, uncompromising, judgmental, and so forth. Still, I thought I might escape, and the problem for me was that Isabel, with certain modifications, *was* all of these, a living, breathing validation of the archetype. What prevented me from truly hating her—what caused me, rather, to squelch the upwelling of extreme dislike that her charmless character traits called forth—was my devotion to my father, whom I loved despite the baffling absence of taste that caused him to choose this homely middle-aged dominatrix for a wife. His love for me was obvious, transparent, and it would have been a body blow to him had I given her the snarling comeuppance I thought she deserved and slammed out of the house for good.

So Isabel and I maintained a frosty politeness and I tried hard to repress my rage at what I conceived to be her irrational antagonism. Likewise, I'm sure she put a stopper on the resentment she felt whenever she regarded her stepson: the ungenerous, self-indulgent, supercilious, arrogant, potentially alcoholic, masturbating, parasitical, egomaniacal young lout who lolled around the house with his balls hanging out of his green marine skivvy drawers. God knows—especially given the emotional upheaval I was going through at the time, my unheroic though spellbinding escape from death, my survivor's guilt, my sexual insecurity—I was no prize myself. Anyway, only a few months after the end of one war I was in another one—a cold war, to be sure, like the one that had begun to engulf the world (just recently annunciated by Winston Churchill at some Missouri cow college) but no less ominous and nasty.

Supine, gazing gravely across my midriff, I blessed the tent-post rigidity that made a modest canopy of the sheet that covered me, and I worked at pushing back the urge to dally a bit. I did, however, give the upright a token stroke, more like a benediction, and saved for the last the luxury of assessing that part of me that took priority over hands, fingers, legs, arms, even eyes—even *brains. Especially* brains! Who needed brains? Marines had shed seas of sweat before a Pacific landing, tormented with fear over the safety of their adored apparatus. Nature had positioned the whole works in a relatively sheltered place; wounds there were relatively infrequent, yet young men in battle had sometimes been converted into instant eunuchs. It was another piece of myself whose survival was something to praise.

Well, just one more squeeze, I thought—a thought that coincided with a flash of flesh (what part of her I could not tell, though she was clearly unclothed); the translucent gauze of her curtained window prevented anything but a rouged phantom that as always nearly stopped my heart. Mamie Eubanks, right on time to the dot, toweling off after her morning shower. The Eubanks house, next door, was disturbingly near, Mamie's bathroom at such close remove from my bedroom window that, were it not for the intervening curtain and its frustrating semi-opacity, my marine sharpshooter's eyes would have been able to discern each pore on her beautifully proportioned twenty-year-old bottom. As it was, the voyeur's anticipation in me, whetted by the sound of splashing water and Mamie's larky voice, usually warbling a hymn, was always ruined by the drapery beyond which she would float, revealing a distant rosiness or an instant's smudge I assumed was pubic hair, and that was all. Most of this to such inspiring tunes as "Blessed Assurance, Jesus Is Mine" or "Shall We Gather at the River."

It was a routine that had gone on for several weeks. My father had moved into a neighborhood which, despite the elegance of the view, would have to be described as "mixed income." He was not rich but richer than his neighbors. The Eubanks family were hardworking and respectable people from some remote rural area across the James River, uneducated, decent folk with whom my father got along amiably, especially since his own origins were humble enough. But as there was nothing much in common between the Eubankses and my father and Isabel, the house next door remained largely an undefined presence and nothing more, though its proximity caused certain vague irritations. Mrs. Eubanks cooked constantly for a tribe of poorer relatives spread across the town, and the smell of her heavy country cuisine—ham, gravy, snap beans, black-eyed peas—often invaded our rooms. We inhaled a perpetual atmosphere of warm collard greens. Mr. Eubanks, a sometime preacher and part-time undertaker, had a deviated septum; his snores on still summer nights, when the windows were wide open, were often vibrant and alarming. On those nights my father, sleepless, would moan and call Mr. Eubanks "King Kong." Mamie Eubanks had become my own personal thorn. When, some years before, I had gone off to boarding school, she had been an awkward and nondescript tyke with an unattractive pink frosting of acne.

Now I could scarcely believe the transformation. In those days the phrase that defined a young woman who had achieved an obvious sexual potential was "sweater girl," and this Mamie was beyond question. Her complexion had the sheen of a gardenia, and beneath the cashmere she was all delicious bounce when she skipped up the walkway next door and sent me an inviting "Hi!" This had been several weeks before, just after she had returned from summer session at some Bible college in North Carolina, and from the instant of our reacquaintance I harbored an ineluctable craving to do with her what I had been deprived of doing for so many months in the Pacific. I was surprised that I'd held off so long. I didn't know whether she was a virgin or not—as a Southern Baptist, member in good standing of the Baptist Young People's Union, she was most likely utterly unsullied—but it excited me to think that discovering whether she really was or wasn't could be part of an imminent erotic adventure. Lying there, I resolved to give her a phone call, as soon as my tumescence subsided, and arrange for a date, if possible that evening. She was of course so close I could just as easily knock on her door and ask her in person, but I was still a bit shy, and the telephone might provide the right margin of distance.

I glanced at the albums which I'd been leafing through

the night before, and had left on the bed beside me just before nodding off to sleep. One of my recent delights had been that of encountering anew some of my boyhood mementos and treasures, items that had been stored in closets ever since I'd gone off into the marines. I'd remembered a number of these possessions at odd moments while on Saipan or on some troopship or other, but I'd never thought I would see them again; to look at them now, to touch them and ponder them, connecting them to mementos of bygone experience, gave me a rich feeling of privilege, as if I'd come back from the dead (which I had) to reclaim objects made immeasurably more precious because they once seemed forever lost. There was my Remington .22 rifle, still rust-free and smelling of oil, which I'd shot squirrels with in the woods near the C&O tracks. There was a set of bound mimeographed editions of the *Seahorse*, the literary magazine I'd edited at boarding school. A silver cup I had won racing my Hampton One-Design, the little wooden-hulled sloop I'd helped build with my cousin. The twelve volumes of *The Book of Knowledge*, published in England circa 1910, which I'd read tirelessly between the ages of eleven and thirteen, brooding over its photographs of children my age on the beaches at Blackpool and Brighton, and playing cricket, and eating things like bubble and squeak and scones and other confections that American boys had never heard of. There were my Charles Atlas lessons, mailed to me weekly during the summer of my fifteenth year, when I was anxious about my attenuated physique and had ordered (for the then-prodigious sum of twenty-five dollars) these dozen booklets, sent at two-week intervals, instructing me in "dynamic tension," a weight-free technique whereby the ninety-eight-pound weakling would grow biceps the size of melons if he opposed his own muscles against each other long enough and hard enough; I had abandoned the regime after the second week, worn out from standing, jockstrap clad, in front of a mirror, futilely pulling and stretching my skinny limbs.

Then there was my album of photographs. On Saipan, during the days and nights when I was most certain that my death was foreordained, I longed for this album with a sorrowful sense of loss I'd never thought possible. The album was the collective memory of my early youth, containing the images of those who had been dear to me, family and friends locked away in a closet ten thousand miles from the island where I was stranded in a near paralysis of fear. And so, having been persuaded that I would never see these likenesses again, much less their flesh-and-blood avatars, I pounced on this tacky leatherette volume with greedy pleasure. Looking at these dozens of snapshots was like re-entry into a boyhood where all my friends and companions had been brought back to life even as I had been granted a commutation from a sentence of death. But because that morning I would not, try as I might, rid myself of a nagging prurient fever, I returned once more not to my boarding school pals or buddies from grammar school days but to my cousin Mary Jane. There she was, four and a half feet tall, too cute for words, mugging shamelessly as she always did whenever I hauled out my Kodak during that summer before the war, in the aftermath of my mother's death, when I was sent to estivate with my nice aunt and her nice state cop husband in a tiny Carolina town just over the border. My stay there, asphyxiatingly lonely, produced one ineffaceable memory: the onset of my hormone supply, like the Johnstown Flood.

I had just turned fourteen. I'd half-forgotten the worst of that interminable summer—the loafing around in the airless bungalow, the radio's hillbilly strumming, the afternoon sacrament of ice cream, the forlorn moviegoing—but I couldn't possibly forget my lust, a brand-new sensation (late bloomer that I was, I'd not begun to practice the Secret Vice) and oddly scary, inasmuch as I found it focused on the loudmouthed moppet of the house, Mary Jane. How could I have such feelings about a *relative*? And one so *young*? Consanguinity, I thought, and fear of incest were supposed to prevent the desires that were overwhelming me for my maddening kinswoman, age eleven, with the Juicy Fruit breath and the precocious boobs who would plop herself, giggling, into my pajama-clad lap and howl, *Momma, Paw-ul's teasin' me!* Little did she know who was teasing whom, nor the effect she had one morning when, prying herself out of my now eager clutches, she innocently grasped my engorged rod and demanded, "What's that?" Hysterically I replied, "I don't know!" and bolted to the bathroom for the sweet cataclysm of my first orgasm. Lucky for us both, no doubt, my sojourn ended soon afterward. But that noisy little hoyden would remain my Circe forever, and Ahoskie, N.C. (pop. 4,810), my unforgotten Babylon.

I heard my father clomp down the stairs on the way to breakfast, and I was about to jump out of bed, as I usually did, throw on my bathrobe, and join him at the table. But at that instant my eye was caught by the copy of the *New Yorker* I'd bought at a downtown newsstand the night before. I had gone to sleep while just beginning to browse through the cartoons and now, plucking the magazine from the pillow next to me, I perceived something I hadn't noticed before, something utterly remarkable. The text of the issue was unbroken from beginning to end, column after column of print weaving through the advertisements, the entire story or narrative or whatever it was marching on inexorably without interruption until it terminated on the final page just above the byline: John Hersey. It was amazing—a whole issue devoted to a single article. I turned back to the beginning and the title "Hiroshima" and began to read:

A NOISELESS FLASH

At exactly fifteen minutes past eight in the morning, on August 6, 1945, Japanese time, at the moment when the atomic bomb flashed above Hiroshima, Miss Toshiko Sasaki, a clerk in the personnel department of the East Asia Tin Works, had just sat down at her place in the plant office and was turning her head to speak to the girl at the next desk.

I kept reading. The structure of the chronicle was clearly established in the first long paragraph: *A hundred thousand people were killed by the atomic bomb, and these six were among the survivors. They still wonder why they lived when so many others died.*

I threw off the sheet and propped the hefty magazine against my belly. I'd read Hersey before. Most literate marines who hadn't seen action had been moved to pity and terror, or were sometimes merely worried half to death, by his reports in *Life* magazine about the grisly combat on Guadalcanal, and now the clear, precise, understated writing that I remembered from *Into the Valley*, which I'd read on Saipan, with its excruciating descriptions of young American troops in the toils of battle, was again on display. Only here the sufferers were Japanese. I was well into the narrative, five or six pages along, reading about a survivor named Mrs. Nakamura, and her remembrance of the blinding white flash that enveloped her seconds before the blast brought the house down in splinters around herself and her children. Just then from below I heard a horn toot and realized it was my father's car pool group waiting on the street. Hersey's account, filled with suspense and portent, had been so absorbing that I'd forgotten about breakfast. I hopped out of bed and threw on a robe, then hurried downstairs with the *New Yorker* in hand.

"Mornin', son. What are you going to do today?" said my father. He was standing at the front door in his shirtsleeves, the jacket of his suit draped over one arm. It was ominously hot, hinting at one of those brutal Tidewater days just beginning to build up a head of steam. No wind stirred on the harbor. A couple of electric fans sent a tepid breeze through the hallway. The mockingbird in the locust tree commenced a spiritless chant, as if already daunted by the heat.

"I guess I'll spend most of my time at the library," I lied, knowing where in fact I most likely would be. "I'm making my way through Sinclair Lewis."

"Well, I'll see you tonight," he said. "I reckon you'll be having lunch downtown." What he meant was that as usual we would not be sitting down for a midday meal together here at home. Many white-collar employees at the shipyard still observed the old-fashioned convention of shunning the few greasy-spoon establishments in town and returning to their houses for lunch. Although the trip required at least fifteen minutes in either direction, the shipyard's liberal policy of allowing its office workers an hour-and-a-half lunch break gave my father the chance to enjoy a fairly relaxed meal with Isabel. Small-town southerners frowned on restaurants in general, and so this noontime routine (abandoned throughout most of the barbaric North, my father observed) was a way of observing a civilized amenity long taken for granted in places like France. But, as my father surmised, I would not be sharing this midday pleasure. Given our prickly relationship, it was hard enough for Isabel and me to get through breakfast and dinner without a spat; the extra meal would be more than either of us could handle. As it was, I truly dreaded breakfast alone in Isabel's company without my father's moderating presence.

"Have a fine day, son," he said, and hugged me with one arm impulsively as he often did. I could almost feel his love flow into me. I often had the notion that he was still in a state of mild shock, as I was, over my return from the Pacific, not wounded or in a coffin but nimble and breathing. And this despite his abiding belief that God would watch over me. I was his "only root and offspring," as he ceaselessly told people, echoing biblical text, and he had prayed long and hard for my survival, telling me in the many letters he wrote me while I was on Saipan that he knew I would return in good shape, thereby affirming more faith in Divine Providence than I myself even remotely possessed. It would doubtless have shattered him utterly had I been destroyed, after my mother's death only brief years before. So when he hugged me the emotion was still intense, and I hugged him back with feeling. Then I watched as he went down the steps to join his fellow cost estimators, midlevel drones whose dogged labor with slide rules and adding machines, however boring, had been essential in producing such leviathans as the carriers *Yorktown* and *Enterprise* and thus helped in disposing of the Yellow Peril.

I had a moment's reverie about those adding machines, and I recalled how utterly devoted he was to his job, often working on his own time and showing up at his office on Sunday afternoon with me in tow. At age ten or eleven I was fascinated by that office. It occupied a grand vaultlike space on the second floor of the shipyard's headquarters and had a view of the acres of industrial area below. On weekdays the yard was truly a satanic mill, throbbing and smoking and aswarm with thousands of black and white workers who out of habituation or indifference seemed unfazed by the inhuman noise. A terrific clanging erupted from the machine shops and foundries, and there were flashes of fire; out of the hidden guts of huge sheds came inexplicable booming noises and the chatter of riveting hammers, while above the dry docks, where great ships loomed, there were soaring cranes that made, intermittently, a mysterious aerial screaming. Steam locomotives snaked their way through the yard hauling freight, and their whistles added to the racket. But on those afternoons of my reverie the whole operation was shut down, perfectly still, as if in the grip of an immense anesthesia, and in the Sabbath hush I listened to my father clicking away on his adding machine and felt stirrings of disquiet, the mild nausea of unfocused dread.

Why this fidget and anxiousness? No doubt the contrast between the weekday bedlam and this Sunday silence. But it was also the workplace itself, a gloomy oblong of aching uniformity, row upon row of desks, each desk with its gooseneck lamp, its ponderous black Underwood typewriter, its Burroughs adding machine. Well before my awareness of Kafka or Chaplin's *Modern Times,* or Karel Čapek's surreal vision of mechanical doom, I sensed that my father's daily habitat was oppressive and slightly inhuman. I was repelled but also fascinated by the adding machines and I would spend the time punching brainlessly at the keys while my father's own machine kept up its clickety-clack, its monotonous computation. I'd wander around the floor, peering into other offices with more rows of identical desks, gooseneck lamps, Burroughs adding machines. In the echoing sepulchral men's room, with a ceiling as high as a church dome, I'd stand atilt at one of the American Standard urinals, in monumental porcelain, and close my eyes, inhaling the smell from the camphoraceous block of deodorant and listening to the water trickling down. *Why am I here?* I'd wonder in a preexistential existential spasm. Back at his desk my father would still be bent over his machine, which unspooled a ribbon of paper tape that reached to the floor. At the office window I'd gaze out at the shipyard's sunlit vastness, at the massive piles of sheet metal, at the foundries and shops where nothing stirred, and, in the distance, the hulls of ships in mid-creation, where the jagged silhouettes of cranes brought to mind the shapes of prehistoric birds I'd seen in *The Book of Knowledge.* The scene overwhelmed me with a sense of my own smallness, and I'd wonder one more time at my father's connection with this majestic undertaking. I only wished, in my secret self, that his job was somehow more heroic, that he might, for example, be an operator of one of those spectacular cranes . . .

This month would mark my father's thirtieth year at the shipyard, and he was proud of having contributed what he called his "mite" to the war effort. From the open windows of the car I heard his laughter, then a high-pitched *No! No!* as he absorbed the gentle ribbing the crew gave him each morning, and I felt another warm loving pang even as I hesitated there sweating a little, ready to face Isabel.

Out of the plastic larynx of the table-top radio, perched on a shelf in the "breakfast nook," came the subdued squawk of the morning news program, largely items of local (or state of Virginia) interest emanating from station WGH, call letters standing for World's Greatest Harbor—more municipal boosterism. Isabel and I exchanged exaggeratedly polite good mornings while she fussed around over the French toast, obviously poised to bring it to the table. I said it was plenty hot. Isabel replied that the weather report predicted ninety-five. I spoke of the humidity: the trouble was mainly the humidity. Isabel said, yes, in someplace like Arizona ninety-five would be bearable. It was such a dry heat there. Even a hundred, I ventured. While we chatted thus, I couldn't help thinking of a climatological fact which my father, always preoccupied with environmental trivia, was fond of pointing out during heat waves: that this area of southeastern Virginia was really, weather-wise, part of a continuum with the Deep South. It had to do in a measure with the influence of the Gulf Stream. That was why, he explained, the region was hospitable to magnolias and cotton and even water moccasins.

"There we are," said Isabel with what seemed genuine friendliness as she slid the French toast onto the table in front of me, simultaneously pouring a cup of coffee. I was encouraged by this touch of benignity. Maybe we could be chums, after all—at least not perpetually geared up for an enervating quarrel. Nevertheless I was a little relieved to no-

tice that she had already had breakfast, which would elimi-
nate the across-the-table chitchat.

While she cleaned up the other dishes, I addressed myself to the French toast ("Delicious, Isabel!" I exclaimed,
adding my own cordial note) and was about to return to the
New Yorker when a name uttered by the radio announcer
brought me up short. *Booker Mason.* Last-minute appeals to
the United States Supreme Court for Booker Mason, the
voice said, had been turned down and the condemned man,
a rapist, would die by electrocution in the state penitentiary
at eleven o'clock this evening. The pen was familiarly known
as The Wall throughout Virginia, and the voice called it that.
I put my fork down and stared at the radio. For days I'd followed Booker Mason's fate in the local gazette. Not that
there was anything dramatically different between Mason's
story and that of the seemingly countless Negroes who had
trudged that Last Mile in Richmond before the war, when
(nearly always over my breakfast cornflakes, just before the
high school bus) I would read with morbid attention of their
demise, more often than not in a disappointingly brief paragraph or two on the paper's inner pages. Occasionally a
white man would go to his doom, but the felon was far more
likely to be black, and I grew accustomed to the somber reports, always feeling a slight visceral thrill at such passing
details as the last meal (usually fried chicken or spareribs or
some other soul food, accompanied by RC Cola or Dr. Pepper) and the last words ("Tell Momma I'm gone to Jesus"). I
had never been much bothered by the rightness or wrongness
of the electric chair, and while I was not truly a death-
penalty enthusiast I possessed, even as a backslid Presbyter-
ian, enough remnant Old Testament vindictiveness to view

that awful 2,000-volt launch into the great beyond as probably a just and fitting exit. I say "probably" because I was not
one hundred percent certain; in the case of Booker Mason
my uncertainty had been bolstered by circumstances that
made me think the problem through with a new emotion—
worry.

What worried me was a matter that had not previously
crossed my mind: the condemned man was not a murderer.
Even the Commonwealth conceded that. The reason Booker
Mason was being put to death was not for causing death but
for sexual violation of a woman—pretty nasty stuff, of
course, a happening of profound pain and degradation, one
regarded universally with outrage and surely occasioning the
need for reprisal but never more urgently than in the black-
belt backwater of Sussex County, where Mason committed
his crime. In that part of the Old Dominion, Negroes walked
lightly and talked small. There wasn't much in mitigation of
the felony since Mason, twenty-two years old and a farm
worker, openly admitted his "criminal assault" (delicate
newspaperese for rape) of the woman—a fortyish housewife
who was also his employer—not only admitting it but, in a
fashion described as "sullen and boastful," declaring freely
that it was at least in part an act of vengeance for past slights
and humiliations. Save for the rape itself the victim was not
physically brutalized; she told the court she had quiescently
submitted out of terror, and there was no attempt on the
part of the defense to suggest seduction on her part since
Mason's own defiant confession effectively ruled out such a
tactic. He had simply, coolly and calculatingly, fucked her,
hour after hour. So this was an instance where even a sympathetic, racially tolerant white person—one accustomed to

a distinct queasiness when a black man was executed despite (as was often the case) manifest innocence, or at least unproven guilt—might compliantly accept the obvious: a bad nigger in bad trouble, richly deserving his last ride on the lightning bolt to eternity.

But I was still worried, and I said so out loud, in a spontaneous outburst. "Jesus! They're putting him to death and he didn't even kill anyone."

Just as I spoke I wished I'd kept my mouth shut, for Isabel shot back from the kitchen: "He deserves worse than the electric chair for what he did. He killed her soul."

The back of my neck prickled in warning. In our many disputes—a few of which had escalated perilously near out-and-out combat, though always falling just short of that—I had tried to assess the tonality of Isabel's voice, learning that some subtle shift of timbre might indicate sudden antagonism toward me apart from the subject at hand. I listened for that tone now, on guard and a touch nervous, not wanting the discussion to turn nasty after our relatively cheerful détente. Her brisk retort to me seemed satisfactorily impersonal, and I might have left it there, dropping the matter. For a moment I really decided to press on, even though there was risk involved. Still, I hesitated, happily ingesting the strong good coffee, which blended in rich harmony with the taste of maple syrup. Terrific, I thought, bidding adieu once again to the Marine Corps' glutinous powdered eggs. I had a mild surge of matutinal euphoria, a mood I would have liked to maintain. I changed my mind: no talk of Booker Mason. Over the hum of the electric fan the radio voice, a plummy drone, intoned the shipping news: arrivals and departures, traffic in and out of the World's

Greatest Harbor. S.S. *General Henry McIntosh,* mixed cargo, bound for Buenos Aires. S.S. *Rio Douro,* pottery and cork, inbound from Lisbon. S.S. *Fairweather,* grain and leaf tobacco, bound for Rotterdam. S.S. *World Seamaster,* coal, bound for Le Havre (the voice pronounced it like a guy's name, Harve). With syrup-sticky fingers I leafed my way through the front pages of the *New Yorker,* found the Hersey piece, and had picked up Mrs. Nakamura's narrative when Isabel added: "They should take a nigra like that, before they kill him, and impale him with a hot poker like he did to that poor woman."

"Oh for God's sake, Isabel," I blurted, "lay off it. The nigra was a monster. He should be put away somewhere to rot forever. But there's a simple fact here. Yeah, the woman was raped, and that's horrible. But she's *alive!*" (I said "nigra" not in mockery of Isabel but because I too, like most educated denizens of the Tidewater, and the South in general, wasn't vocally conditioned to say "knee-grow," and so employed such a pronunciation naturally, in an attempt at respect; Isabel was too well-reared to have said "nigger," the language's most powerful secular blasphemy.) "I'm not entirely sure I don't believe in the electric chair," I went on. "It may be necessary. But it's barbaric to *kill* a man for *rape,* no matter how awful the crime is!"

"You're not a woman," she replied bitterly. "You can have no idea of the lifelong trauma of such an act—it can destroy a woman, body and spirit."

I refrained from responding about the obvious possibility of males being raped, a fact of life of which Isabel, as a nurse with E.R. know-how, must have been well-informed. Instead, ratcheting up the tension a bit, I found myself say-

ing irritably: "You mean *a fate worse than death*?" I paused
for an instant to let the old bromide sink in, meanwhile becoming aware of *her* tension; working away at the dishes,
she had paused midway in a wipe, her fingers trembling, and
a flush had spread cross her broad ill-proportioned face,
coming out in blotches. It was time to cajole her gently.
"Really, you're an educated lady. It doesn't become someone
of your intelligence to hang on to such an idea."

On the edge of a reply she stopped, cocked an ear at the
radio, and we both attended to the latest Booker Mason bulletin. It was more doom. Having exhausted all appeals, the
condemned man's attorney—speaking yesterday evening
from the steps of the state capitol in Richmond—had en-
treated the legislators to use the tragedy of Booker Mason as
a symbol for the need to repeal an inhuman law which made
a travesty of the principles of justice enunciated by such
great Virginians as Patrick Henry, Thomas Jefferson, and
James Madison . . .

"It's just more garbage from that little New York Jew,"
said Isabel in a flat exasperated tone. "He certainly loves the
limelight." Her remark, while fairly typical of her diction,
was not as anti-Semitic as it sounded since Isabel was neither less nor more prone to bigotry than numberless nicely
bred Virginia women of her place and time. She was far less
anti-Jewish than madly pro-everything that Jews were not
and that she was blessed enough to be: an alumna of
Randolph-Macon Women's College (which had enrolled
only Anglo-Saxons) and a member of both the Episcopal
Church and the Tidewater Garden Club, two sublimely Virginian and *goyish* institutions. In fact, giving her credit,
which I honestly tried to do at every turn, I had noted that

from time to time she had spoken with some warmth of various local Jewish citizens whose names cropped up over the dinner table. She was a passionate churchgoer and devotee of the Gospels. Southern Baptists and other lower-class sects might have bred anti-Semites, but her brand of well-mannered Episcopalianism would have not permitted the vulgarity of overt prejudice concerning Jews. Thus, "that little New York Jew" was pretty innocuous, and not so much intolerant as ignorant since the New York Jew in question, Lou Rabinowitz (whose picture in the paper she had not seen, as I had), was actually well over six feet tall, towering above his spindly client Booker Mason, the rapist singled out by the National Association for the Advancement of Colored People as the principal in a constitutional test case. He really did love the limelight, Lou Rabinowitz, with his cape, his ascot tie, and Barrymore profile, but he fascinated me, and as I followed him in the news I perceived that he was bent on turning the justice system of Virginia upside down.

"It's not garbage!" I answered back, a little too loudly. "And so what if he loves the limelight! He's trying to bring this dumb state into the twentieth century!" Rabinowitz's incessantly spouted facts and statistics came pouring out of me. "Did you know, Isabel, that Virginia is one of just five states—all of them southern—that keep the death penalty for rape? And what about this! Did you know that over the years in Ole Virginny four hundred and seventy-five white men have been convicted of rape with *no* executions, while forty-eight colored rapists have gone to the fucking electric chair? It's a fucking scandal!"

"Mind your language!"

"I'm sorry," I said. Daily life in the marines had been so

foul-mouthed that in the aftermath I had trouble curbing my tongue. "I'm sorry but I don't think you understand, Isabel, how *medieval* it is to have such a law!"

Over her face there came a drawn and long-suffering expression I had come to know well. It usually foretold commentary that subtly burnished her own image. "By and large I've had nothing but the most cordial relationship with nigra men. The orderlies at the hospitals where I've served have been mostly hardworking, responsible men with whom I've worked side by side and to whom I've always made the gift of my trust!" ("Gift of my trust." *Jesus!* I thought.) "But you must keep in mind that here in the South male nigras have had some kind of unnatural sexual need to dominate white females—"

"Oh for God's sake," I interrupted, aware that the situation was beginning to veer out of control. From my mouth flew a piece of French toast. Fearful that this morning we might, finally, be at each other's throats, knowing that I'd better throttle back my accelerating rage, I nonetheless helplessly charged on. I threw my napkin down and rose to my feet, overturning the coffee cup *and* the syrup crock, simultaneously, catastrophically, spreading the dark unholy mess across the table. "This idea I just can't bear! This idea in the head of every cretinous blonde in Dixie—that around the next corner lurks a rampaging black beast ready to get into her hot little twat—" I turned and fled.

But I was almost instantly aware of a need to salvage the situation. Standing on the screened-in front porch, pulse pounding and in the throes of hyperventilation, I realized I'd made a mistake. It was I, after all, who had flown off the handle, lost aplomb, and therefore lost the skirmish, and I knew I'd have to make amends. And better now than even a few moments later. I whirled about and returned to the table, whispering my apologies as I clumsily helped her clean up the spill. "Paul, let's just drop the subject," she muttered. I sat down again and gloomily resumed chewing and reading. So I'd *lost* the skirmish. But I felt that neither of us had won or lost important points. We were at our customary tense stalemate.

Silently and, I thought, with a promptness that seemed a little too dutiful, she poured me a fresh cup of coffee. This I sipped with one hand while with the other I flattened the copy of the *New Yorker* and continued reading. I absorbed the early ordeals of Dr. Fujii, Father Kleinsorge, and Miss Toshiko Sasaki: *Everything fell, and Miss Sasaki lost consciousness. The ceiling dropped suddenly and the wooden floor above collapsed in splinters and the people up there came down and the roof above them gave way; but principally and first of all, the bookcases right behind her swooped forward and the contents threw her down, with her left leg horribly twisted and breaking underneath her. There, in the tin factory, in the first moment of the atomic age, a human being was crushed by books.*

The first chapter ended there. It was terrific stuff. Hersey's writing was so chiseled, so detailed, and, in its laconically low-keyed way, so urgent that I had to force myself to stop, knowing I'd be able to savor the rest of the text later on in the day. I got up, uttered a "thank you" to Isabel that was a touch too polite (an unctuousness verging on parody that I really didn't intend) and wandered back out onto the front porch again. The morning was breathless, windless, like the mouth of an oven. Over the vast expanse of the har-

bor there was a curtain of hot shimmering haze. In the channel five or six freighters and tankers, looking like small
model ships from this distance, moved sluggishly toward the
sea. Far beyond them there was a battleship and the outlines
of what appeared to be two heavy cruisers, anchored in the
calm waters off the naval station. I couldn't be sure but the
big one, the leviathan, the battlewagon with its guns jutting
in lethal profile, had the look of the *Missouri*. Hersey's description had left me a little feverish, having tapped into
some fragile ancient memory, and I was struck by an immediate association: only last year, less than a month after the
ceiling fell on Miss Toshiko Sasaki, two of her midget coun-
trymen, dressed ludicrously in top hats and full-dress suits
and looking less like diplomats than undersized undertakers,
had stood on the deck of that selfsame ship—the *Missouri*
now riding on the far horizon—and signed papers ending
the war that nearly ended the life of Paul Whitehurst . . .

I suddenly remembered how fucking scared I'd been,
there on Saipan. I remembered the lagoon beach and the
glorious sunsets sliding down over the Philippine Sea. I remembered, too, how the beach itself was still littered with
the jagged metal junk from the American assault the previous summer, although with caution, pussyfooting among the
rocks and debris, you could always find a decent enough
spot for swimming. The tents of our company bivouac were
laid out alongside a dusty road the Seabees had bulldozed
through the coral after the marines and army troops had
wrested the island from the Japs, months before we replace-
ments arrived. A thousand miles northwest lay Okinawa,

and from that battle the wounded were being transferred from huge floating infirmaries with names like *Comfort* and *Mercy* to the naval hospital not far down the coast from our encampment. Along the road, night and day, a stream of ambulances came with their freight: the gravely hurt, the paralyzed and the amputees and the head trauma cases and the other wreckage from what turned out to be a mammoth land battle.

Actually, I'd just missed the battle. During the landing in April our division had been employed in a diversionary operation—a feint—off the southeast coast of the island. Our presence had been intended to draw the Japs off balance while our other two divisions went ashore (unopposed, as it turned out) on the western beaches. Then we steamed back to the safety, the calm, the virtual stateside coziness of Saipan. Here began to brew my desperate internal conflict. For while the warrior in me—the self-consciously ballsy kid who'd joined the marines for the glamour and danger— lamented not seeing action, there was another, more sensible part of myself that felt immense relief at this reprieve. And reprieve it was. For all of us knew that the invasion of Japan was in the offing and we'd be involved in no more feints or diversions. We'd be in the vanguard. For the first time, I was terribly afraid. And I was ashamed of my fear.

In the evenings we'd spend our last weary moments— our respite from hours of combat training—lolling around in our tents and watching with morbid fixation the parade of ambulances; our eyes tracked these dust-caked vans through a thick haze of cigarette smoke that rose and fell in bluish undulations. My *Pocket Book of Verse*, which I'd lugged around in my seabag all through my Marine Corps career—from the V-12 unit at Duke to boot camp at Parris Island to Hawaii and, finally, Saipan—had bulged out and was close to decomposition in the humid air, but on these evenings I'd lie on my cot and read again from A. E. Housman and Swinburne and Omar Khayyám or some other moony fatalist or master of Weltschmerz, while the tropical dusk would grow murky blue and Glenn Miller's "Moonlight Serenade," or a Tommy Dorsey tune, would sound faintly from a portable record player or radio, drawing forth from my breast a spasm of hopeless, cloying homesickness.

Then I'd get distracted by the ambulances. The caval-cade was hypnotic to watch and just as harrowing. There was a particular hummock of coral that caused the green vans to slow to a crawl, clashing gears as they shifted down. At first these passages over the coral had been uneventful, but the big bump became more ragged and worn away, and I still had the memory of one ambulance that stalled, then jerked back and forth, jostling its poor passenger until the voice from within screamed "Oh Jesus! Oh Jesus!" again and again. I heard screams like this more than once. Poetry was no remedy for such a sound, and so I'd close the book and lie there in a numb trance, trying to shut out all thought, all thought of past or future, focusing on the tent's plywood deck, where usually there was at least one huge greenish snail with a shell the size of a ping-pong ball propelling itself laboriously forward and trailing a wake of mucilaginous yellowish-white slime with the hue and consistency of semen. Great African snails they were called and they slid all over the island, numberless, like a second landing force; they woke us up at night and we actually heard them drag-ging, sibilantly, their tracks across the flooring, where they collided against each other with a tiny report like the cracking open of walnuts.

The fucking snails were always getting squashed beneath our field boots, making a tiny mess that reminded me of the fragility of my own corporeal being. It didn't take long for the instruments of modern warfare to turn a human body into such a repulsive emulsion. Would I be reduced to an escargot's viscous glob? Or did one escape, almost literally, by the skin of one's teeth? One of the riflemen in my platoon, a big muscular farm boy from South Dakota, had seen, strewn on the Tarawa beachhead, a string of guts twelve feet long belonging to the marine who, only seconds before the mortar blast, had been his best buddy. Nearly all the combat vets had endured such grisly traumas. Here during last year's landing on Saipan my new platoon sergeant, a onetime trapeze artist from the Ringling Brothers and Barnum & Bailey Circus, had survived (with only a cut lip and a lingering deafness) the explosion from a Jap knee mortar shell that vaporized the other two occupants of his foxhole. Would I avoid the worst like these guys or would I, when I finally stumbled ashore on the Japanese mainland, be immolated in one foul form or another, consumed by fire or rent apart by steel or crushed like a snail?

Gazing across the water at the distant outline of the *Missouri*, I recalled that stifling tent. Such thoughts had been torment. As I lay on my cot, *The Pocket Book of Verse* would slip from my hand and fear—vile, cold fear—would begin to steal through my flesh like some puzzling sickness. I actually felt my extremities grow numb, as if the blood had drained from my toes and fingers, and the sensation caused me both alarm and shame. Did my tentmates, Stiles and Veneris, the two platoon leaders whose cots lay so closely jammed next to mine, feel the same terror? Did their bowels loosen like mine at the mere thought of the coming invasion? I knew they were scared. We joked, God how we joked—we joked all the time about our future trial—but this was a form of wisecracking, smart-ass bravado, cheap banter. I could never know the depths of their fear. It was a region I dared not explore. In our smothering proximity we shared every-thing else—snores and farts and bad breath and odorous feet. Even the clumsy stealth of jerking off was a matter for shared joking—the unsuppressed moan, the vibrating sheet glimpsed in the dawn light. *Beatin' your meat again, Veneris!* But somehow I knew we could never share real fear. Was theirs as nearly unbearable as mine, this dread that wrapped me in a blanket woven of many clammy hands? Or was their mastery over their fear simple bravery in itself—something I could never possess?

Often I thought it was creepy to feel this fear in such a seductive place. Saipan was really a bowl of tropical Jell-O. Even in the muggy rainy season there were glowing days that made me mourn the recent fate of this lush Technicolor landscape, shattered by gunfire and trampled by so many boots and fires and tank treads. Most of the islands that marines had fought over and secured had been jungle hor-rors infested by disease and rot or were sun-scorched coral outcroppings worthless as real estate and in strategic terms scarcely worth being conquered, much less being the cause of the thousands of American lives destroyed in their cap-ture. But Saipan was actually—I couldn't resist the word—lovable, or would be under peacetime conditions, with a jungle of hibiscus and flame trees and bougainvillea exuding

an urgent exotic odor that was dispersed on balmy breezes
and conjured up visions (whenever I allowed myself to think
the war might ever end) of Pan American Clippers bearing
their cargoes of hot honeymooners panting to get laid or
otherwise to disport themselves in swank palm-thatched
huts on the very beach of our company bivouac. Jesus, I
thought, they'd probably even be getting sex that was air-
conditioned. As I lay in the tent on some mornings, just at
dawn, inhaling the flowered air was like the sweetest aphrodisiac and I'd get tremendously stirred up with lewd fantasies that for a single moment, arresting me in rapture,
would wipe out my fear. It was the merest instant but it
helped. Only a self-induced sexual climax had the capacity
to obliterate the future, and the unspeakable dread of it
dwelling in my heart.

As July wore on, the daily procession of ambulances
dwindled down to one or two every few hours, then ceased
altogether—a sign that the Okinawa battle was now history.
But an ambulance was not the only *memento mori,* and
there were other auguries capable of scaring us shitless. The
word came down through dispatches on the Armed Forces
Radio, and spread rapidly as scuttlebutt all through the encampment, that on the Japanese mainland the civilian population had gone berserk; they were arming themselves to
the teeth—old men, women, and hysterical kids. The Jap defeat on Okinawa, far from crushing the national spirit, had
aroused the citizens to a new resolve, and they'd be waiting
for us with every primitive weapon they could lay their
hands on. On a bright morning after hearing this freakish
news I had one of those strangling nightmares from which
one awakes with heartbeat amok. The dream had a jerky

clarity, like a newsreel clip. In some Osaka suburb I was leading my platoon through clouds of smoke as we roamed about in house-to-house fighting. All of a sudden there rushed at me a murderous little woman in a kimono and with one of those ivory doodads in her hair; screaming banzais and on the point of harpooning me with a bamboo stick, squarely through the gut, she instantly metamorphosed into a nattering wee manicurist busily attending to my nails.

One evening startling news circulated: all the officers in the division were being ordered to assemble immediately in the huge amphitheater at the far end of the beach. Such a muster of officers had never happened before. Almost at once the rumor flew about that we were gathering to learn about the invasion, though precisely what no one could even guess. Just after chow in the mess tent, at around six o'clock, I walked with Stiles and Veneris down a path through a scrubby pandanus-pine grove bordering the lagoon beach and onto the beach itself, a stretch of clean powdery sand cleared of the landing rubble and set apart for swimming. I'd been there many times and so was familiar with the droll monstrosity on the giant poster an engineer outfit had stuck up on a stanchion—a creation executed by some marine who had been a cartoonist in civilian life. It was a bespectacled squinty-eyed Jap soldier portrayed as a dementedly grinning rat. KNOW YOUR ENEMY was the legend beneath the profoundly repulsive effigy complete with shitty-looking cap, buck teeth, whiskers, pink watery eyes, a coiling pink tail, and—drawn with such subtlety that one didn't immediately notice it—an elongated pink cock gripped in a hairy paw. It was this last detail, usually eliciting a slow double take, that got at everyone's funny bone, especially the old-timers who'd been through the meat grinders on Guadalcanal and Tarawa and here on Saipan and whose hatred for the Japs was like an ongoing lust. Aided by the Marine Corps habit of uglifying, whenever possible, the names of natural splendors it encroached upon, the poster had caused this portion of the shoreline to be called Rat Beach, and as we trudged along its edge, mostly silent, I think all of us felt the same desperate unease, aware that in the amphitheater we were doubtless being prepared to receive momentous tidings.

Finally Stiles spoke up. "Jesus, I hope this is it. We wait around any longer we'll go nuts."

Veneris put in: "Maybe they're going to give us a landing date. I hope the fuck it's soon."

I said not a word as all hope withered inside me. *Oh Jesus*, I thought, *I hope the fuck it's never.* I couldn't even work up a falsely brave remark, and I felt twisted with envy at their breezy offhandedness. That wasn't all that I envied about Stiles and Veneris, both of them blandly efficient athletic mesomorphs who could do with maddening grace what I could do only with dogged effort: strip down a weapon, set up a mortar emplacement, follow a compass heading on a night march, quickly find fields of fire for a machine gun, carry out a snappy rifle inspection, even keep their dungarees looking crisp and clean. I wasn't a bad platoon leader; in fact, I was pretty good. I was certainly not a fuckup—I was too desperate to avoid failure and disgrace for that—but in facing certain petty military challenges, duck soup for most lieutenants, I often barely squeaked by. I was happy to be just average. I was happy too that I got along so well with these guys. I'd been boringly and single-mindedly an aesthete in college, a devotee of quality lit and chamber music, with tendencies that might have been known as "neurasthenic." My tentmates had each been standout jocks and were also gorgeous—the blond Stiles on a champion swimming team at Yale; the Greek Veneris, with skin like dark enamel, an all–Big Ten tackle at Ohio State. Such looks and pedigrees gave them a big leg up with the kids in their platoons, while I, skinny and knobby-kneed, almost dared not let my troops see me reading anything so sissified as *The Pocket Book of Verse*.

The amphitheater, a natural coral bowl surrounded by palm trees, was already partly filled with the hundreds of officers and warrant officers of every rank in our division. This vast space served the needs of the army and navy personnel on the island as well as the marines. The week before, Bob Hope had entertained all the troops from the stage, and the week before that we'd sat through an evening of Kay Kyser's Kollege of Musical Knowledge, featuring among other warblers Ish Kabibble and Wee Bonnie Baker, whose infantile voice in a song called "Oh Johnny!" had been one of many dim-witted numbers that had held me captive during my pubescence. If two hours of Kay Kyser had been an ordeal, the same could not be said for Bob Hope; he'd been extravagantly, bigheartedly funny and had brought along a troupe of showgirls, gorgeous long-legged creatures in feathers and G-strings who displayed a stupefying amount of bare flesh as they wiggled their butts down upon the screaming mob. It was another surreal dimension added to this ghoulish Pacific war: the bimbos debarking from gargantuan transport planes, flashing their teeth and gyrating their groins, then becoming almost instantly airborne again, leaving behind thousands of doomed devils with aching gonads. As Stiles observed, the Jap army had at least one thing: they supplied their troops with girls you could actually stick something into.

We waited and fidgeted, minding our behavior. Officers were supposed to exhibit decorum, so we spoke in low voices; when enlisted men had to wait for long they usually became a little raucous and horsed around, grab-assing—it was one of their privileges. I thought I'd managed to dominate my fear but I was wrong. The despondent mood I'd been trying to ward off all day overtook me while we waited, sitting on the hard benches. I was seized by a somber unfocused anxiety; I tried to make it disappear but there was no way I could beat back the waves of panic. I kept talking to myself, falling into a little monologue: *Just stay calm, relax, everything's going to be all right.* Suddenly I saw our battalion commander, Colonel Timothy Halloran ("Happy" was his nickname), take a seat on a nearby bench, and the mere reality of his presence soothed me a bit, as so often happened when he hove into sight. We young officers were all nuts about Happy Halloran, who had a carefully cultivated, corny Irish brogue, a waxed handlebar mustache, a Navy Cross he'd won at the terrible shambles of Tarawa (where, badly wounded, he'd led an assault on a Jap pillbox, killing a slew of the enemy with their own machine gun), and, above all, an intuitive sense of leadership that allowed him to wield strict authority without losing the common touch. Unlike the other services, the Marine Corps has always harbored flamboyant characters and nonconformists, and Happy Halloran filled that bill; we loved him for his slightly wacky heterodoxy, always playfully challenging the System. I happened to glance at the colonel just as he happened to glance at me, and he gave me a wink; I felt a little better.

When at last, long after nightfall, the glittering bright

lights went up on the stage and the presentation commenced, and a parade of high-ranking Fleet Marine Force
officers—big shots from Hawaii—made their speeches, we
began slowly to realize a cold fact: they had nothing new to
tell us. "Security" and "secrecy" were the watchwords. The
assault date was set, announced one intelligence colonel,
but for security reasons it could not be revealed. Another officer took the stage. The site of the invasion of Japan had
been selected, he proclaimed, and the beaches had now
been carefully evaluated for all pertinent factors bearing
upon the successful amphibious landing, but secrecy prevented an announcement of their location. "Then why the
fuck are we sitting here?" I heard Happy Halloran mutter. I
could see the back of his neck redden; he was stewing. A
couple of officers near him snickered. Drops of rain spat-
tered our brows, the palm trees thrashed in the rising wind.
Still another officer from Pearl Harbor, a brigadier general,
spoke from the podium; his gravelly voice boomed over the
loudspeakers: "Gentlemen, we are faced with a difficult
paradox. It would be reassuring if, after the destruction
wrought upon the Japanese army at Iwo Jima and Okinawa,
it could be reported that the morale of their troops had been
shattered, and their resources undermined, making the
coming invasion easier on us. But the plain truth is—and
our intelligence reports are clear on this matter—the Jap
forces are prepared more than ever before to die for the em-
peror, to fight to the last man . . ." He droned on. "More
fucking blather," I heard Colonel Halloran say. "Everybody
knows the fucking Jap cocksuckers are a bunch of suicidal
apes."

Even the star of the evening, an admiral, had nothing
new to say, or rather, what he did have to say was, we all

sensed, ripe hokum. He appeared under the brilliant klieg lights, the first admiral most of us junior officers had ever laid eyes on. His name was Crews. Dressed in khaki, silver stars glittering on his open collar, chewing on a meerschaum pipe, he ambled to the center of the stage with a sheaf of notes clutched in his hand. He was angular and professorial-looking, and he peered at us owlishly through steel-rimmed glasses with lenses that grotesquely magnified his eyes. Plainly he was a desk admiral whose seagoing days were far in the past, and plainly, too, his propaganda mission was to bring us tidings of hope and cheer. Happy Halloran gave a jolly cackle and pounded his fist in his hand as he identified the lecturer, whom he'd encountered before. "I'll be a son-ofabitch if it isn't Good News Crews," he said to those nearby. "The fucking windbag, he's going to feed us the same load of garbage!" And when the admiral began to speak—"Good news, gentlemen!" was his salutation—Halloran muttered hoarsely: "We had this guy just before Tarawa. He told us he had good news. He said after the navy shelled the island it would be a piece of cake. And look what happened!" Halloran needed to say no more. The Tarawa calamity was already a Pacific legend: how naval intelligence, relying on obsolete charts, had miscalculated the tides so flagrantly that the marine troops in their landing vessels were forced to disembark on coral reefs and then wade ashore for hundreds of yards through seas, exposed to killing fire from Japanese machine guns. In the history of warfare no amphibious assault had witnessed such bloodletting. Scores of slaughtered men caused the white-capped waves to turn incarnadine. Small wonder that Happy Halloran detested the navy and its spokesmen. "Listen to this creep!" he said.

"Gentlemen, it's good news indeed," Admiral Crews continued. "I'm here to describe the manner in which naval forces will support you in your operation against the Japanese homeland. Let me say that our support cannot, of course, supplant in any way the marines' incomparable mastery of amphibious warfare, yet we are prepared to make your task easier." He spoke for nearly an hour. He said that while the present war had seen invasions that were complex and audacious enterprises—North Africa, Normandy, Tarawa, Peleliu, Iwo Jima, Okinawa—they would be dwarfed by the magnitude of the coming event, doubtless the mightiest naval offensive in history. He told of the armada of vessels that would be involved—the battleships, the cruisers, the destroyers, the submarines—and the titanic fleet of aircraft carriers with their hundreds of planes, altogether the largest assembly of ships ever set afloat on any ocean. He dwelt on the thousands of tons of supplies the cargo ships would deliver, transported to the Japanese shores from depots across the breadth of the Pacific, from California to Hawaii, the Philippines, Espíritu Santo, and the Solomons. But chiefly the admiral extolled the might of naval gunfire, whose concentration on the landing area, he said, gesturing heavenward with his meerschaum, would be the heaviest ever to support American troops. Together with precision attacks from carrier-based planes, the pre-invasion bombardment would pour fire day after day onto the beaches with such intensity—he paused, weighing the phrase, then said, "with such *stupendous* intensity"—that the very ground upon which the Japanese defenses stood would be entirely obliterated. Furthermore, he added, should the marines be properly apprehensive about underwater obstacles, these would be effectively eliminated well before D-day by teams of naval frogmen who would clear the beaches . . .

"I cannot believe this dingbat!" I heard Happy Halloran burst out, a little too loud, just before the admiral wound down his spiel in a monotonous statistical stutter of tonnages, man-hours, payloads, cubic yards. I could sense a tropical downpour in the offing. Greenish lightning flashed across the ocean darkness, and there was a distant grumble of thunder. Halloran had risen from his bench and was clowning around in the shadows, mimicking the admiral's pipe gestures and delighting the younger officers who, like me, were as much in awe of his maverick brashness, his contempt for the brainless minutiae and hollow trumpery of military life, as they were of his ability to command for himself—when needed—absolute respect. Few senior officers had the capacity to give their troops a big laugh, and the single feature that made tolerable my vision of D-day, if there was such a feature, was having Happy Halloran lead me into the jaws of death.

Now I saw that, having come to the period of questions and answers, the admiral—who appeared slightly deaf—had cupped a hand around one ear and was attempting to answer a question from Halloran; it was a query delivered across the arena in a voice deliberately pitched a little too low for the admiral to hear. Beneath his huge handlebar the colonel's teeth flashed a malevolent grin. The excremental trope was, I thought, stunning: "Are you aware, sir, that you are full of *ostrich shit?*"

It was wonderfully deft in its controlled daring: a lieutenant colonel baiting a rear admiral in public was a scary tightrope act even in a community as notably hostile to navy brass as the marines. The impertinence was astounding, courting severe punishment. But somehow Happy Halloran pulled it off; a ripple of laughter rolled through the crowd of

officers, then became a sustained roar as the admiral persisted with the puzzled "What did he say? What did he say?"
and the wind squall out of the ocean blew stronger, scattering papers and maps and adding its own sudden savage blus-
ter to the general din.

Shortly after this, when the assembly broke up, we
found ourselves running. We were running like hell; that is,
the battalion officers—eighteen or twenty of us platoon leaders and company commanders and a major named Williams,
the battalion exec—were trailing Happy Halloran at full
speed down the hard sands of Rat Beach through a rain-
storm so dense that the water filled our mouths as we ran
and half-blinded our sight. Lightning bolts struck the ocean
and the bordering jungle, and we hollered with alarm. We
ran like maniacs. We were alone in this weird spree; only our
colonel in his dotty genius would have had the gall to lead
his officers on such a gallop after a mind-deadening lecture
and a sixteen-hour day that had already left us aching with
fatigue. But though we were in misery over what was happening, there was not one of us, gasping for breath and
choking on rain, who wasn't somehow secretly proud that
the colonel's inspired whim was testing our endurance to the
breaking point. To patiently absorb this extra shred of suffering was one reason we'd joined the marines. And so, glad
masochists all, we fled down the sand in the darkness, following our dungaree-clad leader with his Jerry Colonna
mustache and his comically off-pitch baritone that suddenly
burst forth with "The Marines' Hymn," which we all joined
in singing, or tried to in the heavy pain of our breathing. I recall thinking what a blessed release this was, what a deliver-
ance from the demons of my fear. If I could be caught up in

pure motion like this, or if, as sometimes happened to me in the jungle, I could stay focused on some knotty weapons problems or question of tactics, I'd manage to keep the terror perpetually at bay. Action freed me. It was only in the quiet hours that I felt the lethal dread.

We halted at last and the weather cleared suddenly and beautifully, revealing a blazing full moon. It was like coming forth from a stifling tunnel. The colonel would have run us on and on into the night, I thought, had it not been for a stone cliff jutting out into the sea; here we came up short and ceased our sprint, utterly pooped. Happy Halloran shouted "Fall out!" and we let ourselves sprawl on the sand, all of us silent for long minutes in the moonlight. None of us had canteens, and our thirst was fierce. Despite the rain we were sweating. The colonel was as bushed as the rest of us. I saw him squatting at the water's edge wheezing hard, cooling his face with handfuls of the surf. After a while he stood up, and when we too began to rise to our feet he bade us stay where we were. He said, "Smoking lamp's lit," and most of us groped for cigarette packs as we tried to find dry matches amid the recesses of our sodden dungarees. Zippo lighters flared in the dark. For minutes no one spoke while we sat there amid the lavender fumes, awaiting what we all sensed had to be a declaration. And as we gazed up at Happy Halloran we saw that the comedian's face had been transformed; he looked back at us with rage and sadness. His lips parted to say something but then, before he could speak, we heard a rumble of engines ascending in the air out of the south. It was a squadron of army air force bombers from the airfield on Tinian Island, across the channel, and they cast down upon us their furious vibrations as they gained altitude and made a slow banking turn in their flight toward Japan. It was known as the nightly milk run. We looked up at their undersides as they climbed over the beach, glimpsed the swollen bellies pregnant with bombs that in some hour of the coming day would be unloosed upon Kobe or Yokohama or Tokyo; the noise was brutal but the planes rose with synchronous grace and when they flew past the moon, hugely silhouetted there, I was reminded of their witches' errand and the awful multitude of deaths down in those paper-and-bamboo cities. It didn't bother me too much since I had caught the contagion of Jap hatred and, anyway, now (as the planes vanished northward) I was ready to hang on to Happy Halloran's every word.

"Never believe the fucking navy, lads," the colonel said. "They will betray you over and over. Before Iwo, the admirals said that rock would be smashed to smithereens. They said those sixteen-inch guns would destroy every living thing on the island, even the rats and ants. But you know who died on D-day and afterward. You know how many thousands of brave marines were destroyed." He began to stroll among us, tapping us gently on our shoulders and keeping up a murmurous flow of talk—talk tinged with a melancholy I'd never heard in him before, yet at the same time there was a note that was confident, reassuring. His presence struck some hopelessly romantic chord in me, and I couldn't help but think of King Harry and those troubled yeoman soldiers in the aching dark before Agincourt. "I'll be brief," he said. "We're all thirsty and tired and we need to go to sleep. But I've got to tell you something. You guys have helped make this battalion the best one in the division, probably in the whole Marine Corps. Your NCOs are magnificent. You have wonderful men under your command, and when this showdown comes you're going to get the kind of performance every battalion commander dreams about." He paused for an instant, then continued: "But I don't want to give you any shit like that admiral. I want to speak the real truth. What we're facing is the toughest fight in the history of the marines and we right here tonight are going to be in the toughest part of the fight. I'm not telling you something new. Every one of you knows that because we were in floating reserve at Okinawa and only made that decoy landing, it puts us number one in line to be the spearhead division for Japan. Furthermore, lads, because this regiment, and especially this battalion, is such a fucking good one, I have almost no doubt that we will be the first to put foot on shore."

I'd more or less been aware of this for weeks, or at least I'd suspected it gravely, like everyone else, but to hear the colonel verify the fact, in effect reading out our death warrant, sent my stomach churning in spasms; I saw some of the other lieutenants stir in the sand, as if his words had gripped them, too, with their desperate meaning. "Japan's a big stinking fortress now," he went on, "and you know from Okinawa what kind of fanatic fighting they're going to put up to the very end. The miserable bastards are fighters whatever the fuck else they are—subhuman, I guess. I don't know where they are but the landing beaches will be as impregnable as any such beaches can be made. They'll have guns zeroed in to blow us apart. But we will have to go in and take that beachhead, even if it means that many of us won't be coming back." The moon cast Happy Halloran's shadow over me, enveloping me in darkness as he drew near, and when I felt his fingertips lightly trace their way across my shoulder it was like a sudden benediction, calming—if only for an instant—my sick disquiet. "I don't have much

else to say, lads, except that I think the world of you people."
After a pause he said again, "I really think the world of you.
When the time comes I know you'll do your best—and that's
the best the Marine Corps has to offer. Which is the best in
the fucking universe. Now let's saddle up and walk home."

For a long time in the early hours of the morning I was
unable to sleep. I lay on my cot staring up at the dark canopy
of the tent, listening to the big spooky moths that every now
and then bumped, with a flicker of soft wings, against the
mosquito netting. Once in a while I'd hear another Super-
fortress rising in the distance from the airfield on Tinian,
and far off down the coast there was the faint steady ham-
mering of a pile driver where the Seabees were building a
new pier. *Hang me! Hang me!* spoke the voice of the machine. Close by, a weird bird kept up a disturbance of flirtatious twitters in the jungle; closer still, beneath me, the
snails on the plywood made their clumsy crackling. I focused on their sounds one by one, as if by distracting myself
long enough I might avoid drifting down tributaries of
thought into those swampy visions that would mire me in
absolute despair. From their breathing I could tell that Stiles
and Veneris were deep in slumber, and this caused me an
even more hyped-up wakefulness; *shit,* how could they sleep,
how could anyone sleep after the colonel's evil prophecy?

> *By brooks too broad for leaping*
> *The lightfoot boys are laid;*
> *The rose-lipt girls are sleeping*
> *In fields where roses fade.*

Under my flashlight's gleam I pored over the cluster of
Housman poems in my *Pocket Book of Verse,* letting the sorrow and resignation take hold of my spirit; there was a note

both stoical and ill-omened in this pastoral requiem, and it mated perfectly with my enervation, my feeling of doomsday. I despised myself for being so spineless and disabled, so demoralized, but I could do nothing to avoid the mudslide slowly enveloping me. Finally I put the book aside and lay gazing upward into darkness. I couldn't fight the fatigue any longer and drifted off into a shadowland where fantasy mingled with dream, and I was soon staring down an abomination: myself on D-day, coming undone. Now I saw myself as a figure in a newsreel, a running target. The beachhead was engulfed in flame. The ramps went down and I lurched forward onto the harsh ground, beckoning the platoon to follow me. I stumbled ashore through clouds of phosphorus and across an undulating terrain traversed by barriers of wire. A Jap machine gun, a Nambu, chattered from the flank and the air was thick with shrapnel, roiling, incandescent; the ground rocked with explosions. I turned to see my men hustling low as they scattered and deployed themselves at the edge of an embankment; some guys were falling now, still clutching their rifles at the instant of their collapse into the sand. I glimpsed white bones and blood, flowing like a sacrament. And just then, frozen with the sight of so much blood, I sank into paralysis. I could make no movement, nor speak a word; in the grip of an overpowering numbness I let my mind shut down. Nearby, one of my squad leaders questioned me with his eyes: *Lieutenant, what'll we do?* Beyond power of thinking, I made no reply. Through billows of smoke I saw my tentmates; I could tell that Veneris on my right and Stiles on my left were advancing steadily with their men. Over the radio I heard my company commander's frantic roar: *Get your troops moving!* But the command was without force, without meaning; it could have been shouted in an unknown tongue. My immobility was complete, as if tendrils of myself had burrowed down and sought root in the soil of Japan, rendering me into brainless vegetation. Yet most intolerably—sickening and intolerable—was the look in the eyes of Stiles and Veneris, who, glancing back as they moved through the visible swarm of enemy bullets, turned upon me their measureless scorn and loathing . . .

Coming awake, awash in sweat, I felt my pounding heart, and I thought I'd made a strangled noise loud enough to arouse my friends. But they still slept. For what seemed hours I lay still, listening to their breathing. They would have to be sleeping, I thought at last, when on that not-too-distant night I would fulfill the promise I'd made to myself and enact the lonesome little farce I'd rehearsed so many times before. I was almost ready. Until this moment, I'd never allowed myself to rehearse the first detail of the plan that would lead me into the jungle. But now I let my arm fall to the side of the cot, and I touched with my fingers the cold metal of the carbine cradled in its rack above the flooring. Beneath my hand the barrel of the weapon was oily and slick, and I caressed its surface for long minutes as if touch in itself were reassurance and consolation. Then I drew back my arm. The thought of the coming night filled my mind like an ecstatic heartbeat. What night it would be I didn't know, only that there would be such a night for certain, and soon—the night when at last I stole out of the tent into the cricketing darkness, and there amid the hibiscus and flame trees destroyed my fear forever.

I detected an auspicious note in Isabel's voice when she called from the kitchen and announced, as I began climbing upstairs, that she was brewing some more coffee. "You'll find it in the electric percolator," I heard her say. "It keeps hot. It's a new Westinghouse. Just pour it yourself if you want some later." A speck of cordiality, a soupçon of warmth— could it be that a golden sunbeam was shining in on the stormy weather of our relationship? I sent back over the banister my thanks and proceeded upward to my room. I was beginning to feel better about my stepmother, ready to shuck once and for all the various recriminations I'd stored up for so long, even those I knew were most justified (including the time I overheard her denounce me to my father, after I came in mildly soused at three A.M., as a "degenerate with paranoid tendencies"). Maybe we could live and let live, and the three of us could form an amiable bond of sorts. God, I hoped so.

Mamie Eubanks had disposed herself—I could see down from my bedroom window—upon an aluminum Sears Roebuck chaise longue in the dinky backyard which adjoined our own. She was wearing a two-piece floppy sunsuit, quite chaste in appearance at a time when postwar bathing attire was just starting to exploit the concept of fleshly exposure; still, I could discern her eyewink of a navel and a nice pink tummy which she was presently smearing with Coppertone. Mamie had splendid legs. She propped up against them a copy of *The Robe*, a bloated wartime best-selling novel about the Crucifixion, and this encouraged me a little about the rapport I hoped we'd achieve, for while *The Robe* (which I'd actually tried to read) was a witless piece of inspirational claptrap written by a preacher (like Mamie's father), it did have pretensions to literacy and was a cut well above the fundamentalist religious tomes I expected her to be absorbed in. We might be able to talk about bookish matters.

Just then, her father appeared. A hulking broad-shouldered man, country-bred, he had a ruddy face and the muscular presence of one who had done much manual labor. I had only talked to him on a few occasions and found him polite and soft-spoken with the gawky reticence of an unlettered pastor from the backwoods of Southside Virginia. I suspect he knew I was an infidel. We'd had very little to say to each other, and while his manners were gentle I also sensed something watchful and tightly wound about him; his eyes could grow murky and his jaw become set and grim. I imagined when the holy spirit of the evangel took a firm grip on his tailbone he could really get worked up into a frenzy, especially about sin; I wouldn't want to cross him. Now I saw him approach Mamie and she, looking up, beamed brightly while he stroked her blond curls with fatherly affection and, after some whisperings I couldn't make out, gave a laugh and said, "Praise the Lord!" That's what they must shout at each other all the time, I thought—that and "God love you!" and "Yes, Jesus!" What a fucking family. As I continued my vigil from my peeping tom's roost I saw her absently hike up the hem of her sunsuit bottom, exposing a fetching amount of upper thigh as she vigorously scratched herself there. For some reason it was profoundly arousing. But it also made me feel like a spy. The heat was becoming truly a menace, and I turned away, thinking I'd try to wash away my lust.

Showering off in my tiny bathroom, I made plans for another summer day. I had once again the foretaste of idleness alternating with creative effort. I actually caught myself joyously shivering in the knowledge of my freedom. It was as if I'd recovered from some near-fatal disease. I still was not used to my leisure. I'd almost forgotten that on this morning

I hadn't been forced to jump out of bed before dawn, nor would I have to stand in jungle mud while a torrent of rain filled my mess kit, or become comatose with boredom at a lecture on foot care, or eat a foul meal of unnameable particulars, or wait in futile nauseous hope for a letter in the mail, or salute some repellent fathead of a captain (of which the marines, despite its high standards, had a few) or . . . the catalog went on forever. Civilian pleasures were like an ongoing rapture. In fact, hardly once in my Marine Corps career, except during those precious few days of leave, had I had the time to saturate myself in a shower, as I was doing now, for as long as I damned well pleased. An old ditty popped into mind: *Hallelujah, I'm a bum . . . Hallelujah, bum again!*

After the shower I dressed in one of my more ample sport shirts and baggy slacks—no more form-fitting khaki, binding at armpit and crotch. I glanced at the telephone and was instantly galvanized into a decision. Mamie Eubanks. Any further delay would cause me to lose my resolve for good. While gawking again into Mamie's backyard I dialed her number, indelibly memorized, then simultaneously heard its ring and saw its summoning effect on Mamie; she leaped up, threw *The Robe* on the ground, and scampered into the kitchen. I developed a fist-sized lump in my chest and began to breathe in deep unnatural inhalations. I was so afraid I might betray my feelings—my nervousness, my fear, my unseemly hots—that I was on the verge of slamming down the receiver when I was stopped by the sound of her chirpy voice: "Eubanks residence. Good morning."

"This is Paul, Paul Whitehurst," I said. "Howya doing, Mamie?"

"Paul? You mean Paul next door? Oh Paul, I'm glad to hear from you!" The tone was encouragingly receptive.

"I just thought I'd call you up." My throat produced an unseemly tremolo as I spoke. "Your momma told me the other day that you'd be back from wherever it was you were. Was it down in Carolina?"

"Yes, I was in summer school at Bible college. Out near Boone, in the mountains. It was so cool there. I can't believe this heat, can you? It's like a furnace."

"Weatherman said it was supposed to cool off a little late in the afternoon." I hesitated, then pressed on: "Look, Mamie. I was wondering if you might not be free tonight. We could have a bite to eat, go for a ride."

There was long, rather intimidating silence. Finally she said: "I don't know, Paul. I'd really like to. But my daddy likes me to be home early."

"How early?"

"Ten o'clock." She's twenty years old, I thought, and her old man's still keeping watch like a Weimaraner.

"Well that's all right," I replied. "I could get you back by then." I had begun to gain confidence.

"Also," she went on, "I've got choir practice at five-thirty. I wouldn't be able to get away till seven."

Three hours for fun, or whatever. We discussed the matter in detail. I began to feel better. Despite the impediments she was placing in my way, I was relieved that my scheme was falling smartly into an operational mode. I could still pick her up at the First Baptist Church (where I might dally long enough to see her in her robes, watch her lovely face uptilted as she sang "What a Friend We Have in Jesus" or perhaps "Leaning on the Everlasting Arms"), cruise by the

Peninsula Drive-In for a hamburger, and yet have time enough—an hour and a half, perhaps two—to park at the secluded overlook by the World's Greatest Harbor, where, on the broad front seat of my father's secondhand but immaculate Pontiac, I would become more closely acquainted with this creature. For there was no doubt about it: she had me hopelessly snared, and I could scarcely believe that I'd let myself fall for a dewy Christian seraph. All my wiser instincts told me that I was headed not for bliss but its antipodean double—trouble—yet I could not help myself. "Mamie," I said, just before hanging up, "I'll see you at the church at seven."

"God bless," she replied, disheartening me.

Before heading downstairs for a cup of Isabel's coffee I rummaged through my dresser drawer and placed certain items in my pockets, preparing for the daily foray into town. Handkerchief, cigarettes, Zippo lighter. I'd recently bought a new Swank wallet to replace the one I'd hung on to out of sentiment but for sanitary reasons had had to dispose of: months in the Saipan boondocks had made its crevices crummy with an odorous green mold. Into the new model I slipped a crisp new twenty-dollar bill, which should last me for most of a week, especially since my drinking spot down in the center of town still soaked its customers only five cents for a large glass of draft beer, ten cents for a bottle. Financially, I could hardly be regarded as a plutocrat, though for a bachelor I felt solvent enough owing to the largess of the government; veterans like me who belonged to what had been dubbed the "52-20 Club" received a check for twenty dollars each week for a year, payoff of sorts by the U.S. Treasury Department for getting out of the mess alive.

I put the wallet with the twenty dollars in my hip pocket, and as I did so my eyes lit upon one of the three souvenirs I had brought back from the Pacific. Marines, crazy for Jap souvenirs, scavenged mementos of all descriptions from the gore of the battlefields: Samurai swords, flags, I.D. bracelets, officers' pistols, fancy leather belts, watches, rifles, combs, rice bowls, almost anything one could yank off a corpse.

Some keepsakes were particularly loathsome—gold teeth, dehydrated body parts such as fingers and toes, acquired by the few marines most likely capable themselves of atrocities. I knew a corporal of my battalion who carried with him two prunelike talismans—the dried testicles of a soldier he had personally dispatched in the frenzy of battle on Tarawa. He didn't seem to me a monstrous sort though, and in fact I thought him rather nice; saving a couple of Jap's nuts was really the expression of a marine's immeasurable hatred of the enemy—a hatred felt by nearly all marines—which most stateside Americans could not fathom.

I had acquired a shiny bayonet of tempered steel. Also a flag with the Rising Sun. But my most valued souvenir was the small round locket I'd won one steaming night on Saipan in a poker game. Luck alone might not have accounted for the prize—I wasn't all that sharp a poker player—but the loser of the locket, a regular warrant officer from regimental headquarters, was half-pissed from a bottle of Gordon's gin he'd won that same night in another game and so gave up the lovely bibelot on a dopey call. The locket was worth winning. It was exquisite: burnished gold inlaid with an ivory Jap ideograph in filigree and suspended by a delicate chain. It had a nice heft and a satiny feel when I stroked it. For a long while, rather stupidly, I had thought it to be a solid object, not noticing that it opened up as lockets are supposed to do and in this case revealed a photograph. It was a snapshot taken on a ferryboat. Two little girls who appeared to be sisters—I judged about four and five years old—gazed over the back of a deck chair; they wore identical straw hats with bows tied at the front, and they looked like owlets with their eyes solemn and depthlessly dark.

The picture at first disturbed me; I came close to gouging it out and throwing it away. It added a measure of squeamish self-reproach to the discomfort I already felt at owning such a memento, with its hint of the macabre. But to destroy the charming portrait was an act of such self-conscious guilt that it seemed absurd; the empty space would be an even greater reproach. So I kept the picture in the locket and from time to time stole a peek at the ferryboat children, always making my mind an absolute blank whenever my thoughts began to stray toward the father from whose dead neck my trophy had been torn.

Downstairs Isabel had retired to the alcove off the living room that served as a kind of makeshift office. She was not an idle housewife. As a part-time occupation she still taught nursing at the nearby hospital, which kept her busy with written examinations and paperwork, and she also seemed to spend many hours doing what I gathered were benevolent things for the Episcopal Church; as much as she pained me, and as unbearably narrow as I viewed most of her perspectives, I had to concede that her heart was sometimes in the right place. She believed in charity, not only because her church plumped for the eleemosynary spirit but because (it was like swallowing nails for me to admit it) she did have an impulsively generous side; this took such an elemental form as feeding any of the stray cats that roamed the neighborhood or, in fact, feeding me—after all, she didn't have to bestow upon me the good breakfast I had just downed that morning. I felt like a shit (for an instant) for so grudging her occasional moments of grace; the sound of her fingers devotedly clacking away at her typewriter gave me a twinge of what might actually have passed for lovingkindness.

But it was just a twinge and over immediately. I poured a cup of coffee from Isabel's new Westinghouse percolator. Listening to the voice of Lou Rabinowitz on the radio—the voice of Isabel's nemesis—I realized that her New York Jew had managed to achieve a promotional coup perhaps unprecedented in the Old Dominion. For surely never before in the annals of Virginia crime—at least in the annals of those four dozen Negro men who over the decades had shambled to their extinction for having forcible sexual congress with a white woman—did a wretched felon find such a champion as Lou Rabinowitz. It was he who had summoned the chutzpah to get Booker Mason on the front pages and cause the notoriously reactionary Virginia media to publicize what he called the "monumental" injustice about to take place that evening in Richmond. And he plainly relished his champion's role. His voice had the querulous tonality of the Bronx, along with all the dental consonants, but it also possessed the rabbinical fervor of a man who was descended (as he was quick to point out in regard to his name) from a long line of rabbis.

"What, then, is the next step, Lou?" asked the male interviewer.

"Since the Supreme Court has once again abdicated its responsibility, we have only one option left and that is to request that the governor grant clemency."

"Do you think there's any chance of that?"

"The governor is a man of compassion and a Christian gentleman. His record in granting commutations is better than average among southern governors, in cases where there has been a miscarriage of justice. And this is the worst miscarriage of justice you can imagine."

"Then you think there is something wrong with the law as it stands?"

"I think there is something inherently evil in a law which inflicts the death penalty upon a man for sexual intercourse, even when it is not consensual. When in fact it was forced. I do not pretend my client is a saint. Mr. Mason is admittedly guilty of rape but not of murder or even a degree of manslaughter. Furthermore, Mr. Mason is about to suffer the supreme punishment for a crime for which no white man in Virginia has ever been executed. This is a moral obscenity."

I felt a spinal tingle as I realized that, almost at the same time, my ears had experienced two "firsts": the scabrous phrase "sexual intercourse," which I'd never heard spoken on the radio before, and the simpler word "mister," an honorific so rarely preceding a Negro's surname that it sounded like a joke. Meanwhile Isabel, attracted by the voice of Rabinowitz, had moved toward the breakfast nook and now stood with her head tilted for the interview. Her face wore a look of grim disapproval, and I immediately regretted that the garrulous lawyer with his blunt heresies might get her goat again, thus disturbing the morning's ticklish composure, the balance of our delicate accord. I had the vain impulse to turn the radio off.

"Listen," Rabinowitz was saying, "I keep insisting that the guilt of my client is not in dispute. In a reasonable disposition of Mr. Mason's case he would be given a very long term of incarceration which would satisfy the Commonwealth. Rape is not countenanced lightly in any state in the Union. But I don't want to hide the fact that aside from the aforementioned miscarriage of justice there are matters of principle involved here. We are determined to break down historical prejudices which for centuries have kept Negro men chained in fear. Since the time of slavery the sexuality of white women has been used as a way to tyrannize Negroes—"

Had Rabinowitz's words been poisoned darts soaring across the ether from Richmond to embed themselves in Isabel's broad face she could not have reacted with more instantaneous pain and outrage. "He's a liar!" she shrilled. "What tyranny? Everyone knows the truth about nigra men! This Mason is a perfect example! I mean, the little Jew's client! He flat-out admits that this Mason just cynically and brutally had sex with that poor woman, whatever her name is—thank God they never reveal it—just to get back at her for some imagined insult! He admits it and in the same breath implies that white women are at fault for their own victimization—"

"Isabel!" I intercepted. "He's *right!*" Thinking even as I spoke: *I've got to get the fuck out of this house.* "He's trying to emphasize a larger truth, don't you see? He's not trying to get Mason off the hook; he says that over and over. Nor is he blaming white women. He's merely trying to say that there's

a horrible, unbearable tragedy taking place down here in the
South in 1946, and Negroes are getting crucified as usual
for sins committed by white people." Suddenly I let my
mouth get away with me. "Why in the hell can't you be a little more *tolerant*!"

She was glaring at me. Her eyes were naturally protuberant and whenever she became roiled, as she was now, they
appeared close to popping from their sockets. When I got so
utterly fed up with her (and I was *really* getting fed up) I felt
grateful that she was not beautiful; as it was, a small but real
upwelling of pity, pity for the blotched and homely face she
presented to the world, tended to moderate my rage and prevent the showdown that might have ensued had the old man
hooked a broad a bit more attractive. And a showdown was
what I desperately wanted to avoid. *God,* I didn't want a
showdown. Thus the solemn liberal piety I had just uttered,
even with its severe coda, was really a quickly contrived sub-
stitute for the massive verbal bludgeon which had in truth
nearly escaped my mouth, scarily.

She still glared at me. And I, sending back a prolonged
counterglare, set down my coffee cup, wheeled about, and
strode again to the front porch. My mouth was parched. I
felt all my limbs quivering, and the stress had sent an aching
jolt of adrenaline to my kidneys. The porch was like a steam
bath. While once more I strove to calm myself I spied my father's binoculars; I began to scan the harbor, more as a di-
version, an escape from Isabel, than anything else. The
Missouri swam into sight, so clear now and well-defined that
I could see the white caps bobbing on the heads of the
sailors swarming along the decks. Farther north, toward the
entrance to the bay, a freighter churned sedately seaward; it

was a Danish vessel, I could tell from the large white MAERSK emblazoned on its side. The bold letters were not all that common on merchant ships, and for a moment I was put into mind of another ship with a vivid startling emblem, cruising across the harbor many years before. As I walked with my father along the seawall my eyes had picked out a bright red globe on the side of a freighter; even at ten I knew that a ship riding so high was carrying no cargo, and I pointed it out to my father with a question. "It's a Japanese merchantman," he said, and his voice was edged with contempt, or perhaps anger. "That's what they call the Rising Sun on the side. That ship's going up the James to Hopewell and take on a load of scrap iron, or maybe nitrate, or both. Either way, it's a crime." I asked him to explain and he replied: "The nitrate they'll use to make gunpowder, the scrap iron they'll use to make guns. And both of these they'll use on American boys someday, when we're at war. It's a crime, son." I remember him pulling me close. "I got half a mind to write our congressman, tell him we're supplying the enemy." Could he have been thinking, even then, that his only offspring might someday meet the Japanese in battle?

Prescient though he was, I doubt that he actually foresaw his little boy grown up to be a marine leading his troop of doomed warriors into some distant Armageddon; still, he had a good amateur historian's nose for future catastrophe and was aware, as most of his fellow office workers were not, that the gray behemoths he helped build and that had begun, at almost yearly intervals, to slide down the ways into the muddy James were not meant for show but would someday be floating platforms to launch aerial raids on the wicked troublemakers of Europe and Asia. He was hardly an intellectual, but he had read much about war and its politics; for thirty years his involvement with the making of warfare's potent machinery had led him to the conviction that such expensive gear couldn't be allowed to rust. And on the dreadful day of Pearl Harbor, when I called him excitedly from boarding school, I was struck by the dark sorrow in his voice but also by the absence of surprise.

When I set the binoculars down I glimpsed close by, hurrying down the sidewalk bordering the beach, a familiar figure: moving briskly in the heat, it was a phantom from yesteryear. *Good God*, I said out loud, *it's Florence*. Diminutive, hunched over in a white hospital uniform, she was trudging along at surprising speed, and I was a little breathless after I hustled down the porch steps and finally caught up with her. "Flo," I said. "Flo! It's Paul, remember me?"

She stopped and turned about, an old Negro with gray hair gone almost white, her expression a little perplexed, the yellowish eyes soft and ruminant. Tiny blisters of sweat covered the black brow. Suddenly, recognition washed across her face like light. "Paul, Paul!" she exclaimed, and then gave a glorious whoop of laughter. "Lawd have mercy, it's really you!" We fell into each other's arms.

"Let me hug you, sweetie!" she said in a muffled voice, then drew back to appraise me. "I can't believe it's really my little Paul."

"It's me, Flo," I said, "it's me. Come back to the land of the living. It's so good to see you! What on earth are you doing in those white clothes?"

"I started workin' at de hospital last week," she replied, jerking her head toward the red brick building down the harbor. "I gits off de bus on Locust Avenue and I walks by yo' house every day. I only works mornins. Ain't a day goes by I don't think of you, passin' by de house." She looked me up and down. "My my, you is some big boy now. I always thinks of you as jes' a little skinny ol' thing. But Lawd, chile, you has *growed*!" She hugged me again, clasping me to her warm and nurturing self as she had so often during the ten years and more of my boyhood when, laboring in the house during my mother's long illness, she had acquired the mantle of my mother's surrogate, feeding me—sumptuously—keeping me clean, acting as nursemaid and benign disciplinarian, as quick to chastise me for truly rotten behavior as she was to loyally connive at my minor wrongs, sheltering me from parental anger with artful lies. Florence—or Flo, as I called her—had toiled six days a week (excepting only Thursday afternoon) from early morning until far past dark, when she joined the throng of shabbily dressed Negro women stomping down kitchen stoops all over the town, each clutching paper bags of supper leftovers or a can of Campbell's soup (in a process called "totin' ") that augmented their weekly salary of three dollars.

It was Flo and her sisterhood that often waited patiently in pouring rain to deposit three pennies in the trolley car's coin box or, later, when buses began their routes, a nickel, to reach the ramshackle enclave whose boundaries were made evident as soon as concrete and asphalt gave way to rutted dirt. It was only quite recently, in the creeping dawn of a new social awareness, that the section more or less ceased being called Niggertown. She'd been born in the past century on a long-gone-to-seed Tidewater plantation, the ninth daughter of ex-slaves and the thirteenth child born out of twenty, and to me it had always been a miracle that, having had no schooling, she had learned to read reasonably well and even to write, her scrawled messages possessing both a mannerist charm and a hilariously cryptic profundity. All of a sudden, staring into that lively wrinkled face, I was swept by two emotions in excruciating conflict: love, intense love for this sweet shepherdess of my childhood, and shame— shame that in the many months of my homecoming I had neglected to seek her out.

"I was three years in the Marine Corps, Flo," I said. "They put some weight on a guy."

"I heard you was a marine," she replied. "Dat is some bunch of brave boys. Did you git yo'self hurt?"

"No," I said, "nothing happened to me. But I was a long long way from home and I really got lonesome."

"Did dey feed you good? Bet you didn't get no fried chicken with giblet gravy like Flo used to fix you!" She grabbed my arm and squeezed it, with a tickled hoot. "When you was little you could tuck away mo' fried chicken an' rice than three grown-ups. Je-*sus*!"

"I kept dreaming of that chicken. I was on this island out in the Pacific called Saipan. Not a day went by that I didn't think about your fried chicken."

"How's yo' daddy?" she asked, and her eyes grew filmy and tender.

"Oh, he's fine. Still working in the shipyard. Still keeping up the same old grind. He likes what he's doing, you know, Flo. He loves his ships."

"I misses Mr. Jeff. I misses yo' daddy." Her words gripped me with a feeling of loss, and also resentment. Once again— Isabel. For after my mother's death Isabel's arrival on the do- mestic scene had guaranteed Flo's almost immediate exit; it was an abrupt vacuum that created in me near bereavement when, returning from boarding school one Thanksgiving, I discovered that my beloved mammy (if I dared use the obsolescent word) was banished forever. "A hopeless personality clash, Isabel versus Florence," my father had explained, trying to comfort me. "Each of them just too set in their ways."

Now I should have known better than to bring up her name. "He seems happy with Isabel, Flo. She knows how to take care of him."

Flo glowered suddenly and there was acid in her voice. "Hmpf. Dat lady ain't got no soul, chile. No soul at all. You lucky you was a marine."

I changed the subject. "So what are you doing at the hospital?"

"Ise an attendant for de old folks," she replied with a slight air of mockery. "I does de bedpans and I cleans up de barf. Dem old folks is always barfin' everywhere. But I has to make some money. My two boys is over in Portsmouth at de navy yard, and dey gives me some money but it ain't much." As she spoke I felt pain at the thought of her comedown in dignity—the truly inspired culinary artist, the onetime chatelaine of a tiny but contented household brought so low, squatting on her hands and knees upon a grungy floor, swabbing up barf. "But I makes do," she added.

"Well listen, Flo, I hope to see you sometime, I really do. I have thought of you so often and I just failed—" I broke off in embarrassment. "Maybe we could get together."

"Oh Lawd, chile, I'd love to see you. Ise home every day excep' de mornins. Same old house. I ain't got nothin' to do except listen to de radio. I loves my soap operas. *Life Can Be*

Beautiful, Guidin' Light, Right to Happiness, all of dem."
She gave a giggle. "Ise a soap opera fiend."

I hugged her again and then she turned and was gone
toward the hospital, leaving me in a fierce momentary tussle
with anger and the blues and dealing with a crowd of memories. Then I gave thought again to my morning schedule.

Parked on the street outside the house was my father's
Pontiac. The car, which was at my disposal most of the time,
was central to the routine I'd established for myself that
summer. Most mornings I'd drive up to a pleasant neglected
park on the James River, a quiet place where enormous hov-
ering sycamores provided a dappled shade for some rickety
but functional picnic tables. There in this nearly deserted
space I'd sit with a yellow legal pad and a bunch of sharpened pencils and scribble away at what I deemed to be my
"creative writing"; the awkward but heatedly felt short stories I was setting to paper were the result of the authorial
virus I had contracted my first year in college, leaving me
with a chronic fever that plainly was not about to subside.
I'd been emboldened to further effort—no, it was sometimes
a quiet delirium, so high were my hopes—by the not quite
acceptance of a sketch I'd submitted to *Story* magazine, that
paragon among short-fiction outlets, whose reader had ap-
pended to my rejection slip the electrifying postscript *Do try
us again!* How intoxicating to me were the exclamation point
and the imperative quality of that superfluous "do"; for days
I repeated the words like a mantra. I took novels along with
me—Steinbeck, Sinclair Lewis, Cather, Wolfe. Alternating
writing and reading made the mornings pass quickly, and
there was always the mesmerizing prospect of the James, six
miles wide here at its mouth and a river so much a part of an

essential chapter of American history that even I, who all my young life had swum in it, sailed upon it, caught crabs in its shallows, even once nearly drowned beneath its brackish waves, could find myself freshly amazed at the fantasy it evoked.

There was scarcely a time, gazing out on that expanse (too sluggish and muddy to qualify as majestic but still a serious waterway), that the freighters and tankers lumbering upstream didn't vanish before my sight and a single tiny vessel float into view: that Dutch galleon tacking against the wind, heading for Jamestown with its chained black cargo. In a classroom moment I would never forget I listened to Miss Thomas, our distant and opaque sixth-grade teacher, blurt out part of a history text (*In 1619, known as the Red Letter Year at the new English settlement, a shipment of slaves arrived, transported from Africa . . .*), never taking her eyes from the book, her voice a mechanical mumble, the bland-faced spinster completely oblivious of the great stream just outside the window which had borne this craft to its cosmic destination. *Wasn't it right out there?* I called out suddenly, interrupting her, startling my classmates. *Wasn't what?* she replied, startled too. *The Dutch ship that brought the slaves.* For an instant I'd seen it, the galleon, its cumbersome hull high in the stern, dingy, sails set, wallowing westward through the river's undulant swells. *Why yes,* she said firmly, *I suppose so. I suppose it was out there.* She returned to her page, obviously annoyed. The kids whispered together, eyeing me suspiciously. I felt a sudden flush of embarrassment, wondering at the apparition on the river, and at the reckless, almost angry compulsion that had caused me to try to make my dull-witted teacher come alive to the spirit of the past spooking this ancient shoreline.

I couldn't explain why, but Negroes and their teeming presence in my boyhood—the whole conundrum of color and slavery's cruel bequest—had begun to absorb me, battering on my imagination and forcing me to express the mighty grip that black people had on my heart and mind, moving me to scratch it all down in the apprentice stories I sweated over day after summer day at the picnic table by the James. I had just embarked on a trip to Faulknerland—*Light in August* was my first exposure to his stormy rhetoric, and I was smitten. My God! I saw immediately how riven by the torment of race this writer must have been, from the very dawn of his life. He intimidated me with his talent, to the point of making me wince as I marveled at his incantatory rhythms; I knew I could never approximate his gifts, or the surging energy, but the great tragic themes he tackled—of race and mingled blood and the guilt imprinted on the souls of white southerners—were ones that challenged me, too.

I'd work for three or four hours on my raw little tales—about Lawrence, my favorite black barber, or the wisdom of Florence; or once, in an essay in horror far beyond my depth, about a lynching in North Carolina my father had witnessed as a boy—and then by early afternoon it would be time to call it quits. Time to collect my yellow sheets and my two dozen pencils worn down to the wood, to clean up the cigarette butts I'd left in a litter around the picnic table (compulsive tidiness—"policing the area"—fostered by the Marine Corps), to recap the thermos of coffee I always brought along to help jog up my brain cells—all this before driving downtown to the Palace Café for a bite to eat and the pleasure that was, quite simply, my greediest anticipation.

I loved the Palace Café. And I loved getting drunk there. Its therapy lay in the power of the four or five beers that I guzzled to ease, almost after the first half bottle, the racking misery of my time in the Pacific. That time was never entirely absent from my thoughts, creating a constant gripe in my psyche like a throbbing gut; the effect of a few swallows of the good suds was as analgesic as a shot of morphine. It was what the rustic folk of the Tidewater called a "high lonesome," this daily bender of mine. It was a gentle, civilized bender, solitary, introspective, mildly (not maniacally) euphoric, and always cut short before the onset of confusion or incoherence. I prided myself on a certain drinker's discipline.

The Palace Café was a barnlike tavern on the town's main drag; the blue-collar shipyard workers who were its chief clientele, and who dined on its pork-chops-and-potatoes menu, had usually cleared out by the time I arrived, a little after two in the afternoon. I seated myself under an outsized electric fan that stirred the heavy air, odorous with pork. I had the place more or less to myself then, and I would dreamily relax in the same greasy booth, listening to the jukebox and its grieving and lovelorn country troubadours—Ernest Tubb, Roy Acuff, Kitty Wells—who could pluck at my heartstrings with fingers different from those of Mozart but, in their own way, almost as deft and seductive. They, like the cold astringent beer, caused the Pacific and its troubles to gently recede, even as ornate daydreams of the future filled their place. It was like a rage: I *knew* I must become a writer! So I'd sit there and reread my sketches, buoyed toward a vision of myself ten years hence, or twenty, when my work had flowered, then fully ripened, and the fumbling novice had been crowned with the laurel branch of Art. While adrift in these largely deranged fantasies I made a concession to the needs of nutrition by lunching on potato chips and pickled pigs' feet, the latter a specialty of the house.

And then there was my favorite waitress, Darlynne Fulcher. Part of the appeal of going to the Palace Café was Darlynne and her flirty lewdness, a lewdness neutralized by her (to me) advanced age—she was well past forty—and by her truly daunting looks: big porous beak, spectacles, top-heavy hairdo, the works. A nice voluptuous body offset this enough to make plausible her raunchy style, though at the outset I must have sat in my booth five or six days running, taking scarcely any notice of her, before I heard her murmur, as she plopped down a beer: "You look like you need some pussy." It was not at all a come-on; in fact, I realized it was a way to break the ice, to good-naturedly test the bounds of my dogged solitariness. Actually I welcomed the intrusion, since I enjoyed Darlynne's simple-hearted fooling around about sex ("I bet you got a good-sized dick on you, guys with prominent noses are well-hung"), while at the same time she understood my basic need to be let alone, immersed in my remedial bath of Budweiser. In the moments when we did talk, during the late afternoon hours as she'd stand there, hands on one hip, patiently shooing away the flies, I discovered that some intimate communion we'd established made it possible for me to say a few words about the war. What I had to say wasn't much though it was more than I'd spoken to anyone before, certainly more than I'd said to my father or Isabel.

"From the first time I seen you sitting here I knew something was eating at you. It's the war, ain't it? Did something happen to you?"

The question required some rumination. "Well, yes and no, Darlynne."

"I don't mean to pry, you know. My cousin Leroy was shot up real bad over in Europe. He doesn't like to talk about it either."

"No, I wasn't shot. I never got shot at. It was something else I'd had a problem with." I halted. "But I'd better not talk about it." After another pause I said: "It was in my head—my mind. It was worse than being shot at."

She plainly understood my wanting to drop the subject. "How come a nice-looking boy like you don't ever have a girl-friend?"

"I don't know. Most of the girls I used to know—the college girls—are away for the summer. Gone to places like Nags Head or Virginia Beach. Or they have summer jobs in Washington or New York. Anyway, they're gone."

"College girls won't give you a good time. You need a real horny country girl. My baby stepsister's just broke up with her husband, this jerk. She's hot. She really needs a good time. I'm gonna fix you up with Linda."

It hardly mattered that Linda never materialized, content as I was to sit with my amber bottles and my fantasies, my pumped-up auguries of future glory, and with the thrill of the woeful rapture that always seized me when Ernest Tubb's steel guitar struck the first chords of "Try Me One More Time."

Outside I could see the late-afternoon shoppers hurrying homeward. Gathering up my manuscripts I'd give Darlynne a hug, swat her on her big rump, and head homeward myself, steering the Pontiac with focused care, untroubled, optimistic from head to foot, deliciously tranquilized. I'd be going back to college soon, and this dismal battleground would be forever behind me.

ELOBEY, ANNOBÓN, AND CORISCO

Elobey, Annobón, and Corisco. These form a group of small islands off the west coast of Africa, in the Gulf of Guinea, and I pondered them over and over again when we returned to Saipan, where I would lie in my tent and think with intense longing of the recent past—that is to say, my early years.

During the philatelic period of my late childhood only a few years before, a phase that followed my obsession with raising pigeons, I had somehow come to own a moderately rare stamp from "Elobey, Annobón, and Corisco." By moderately rare I mean that the Scott catalog priced the one I owned, a used specimen, at $2.75, which in those Depression days was a large enough sum to make a small boy's stomach squirm pleasurably, totally apart from the aesthetic pleasure of the stamp itself. A note in my album revealed that "Elobey, Annobón, and Corisco" was under the governance of Spain, more specifically Spanish Guinea. The stamp portrayed a "vignette," as Scott always described the world's scenic views, of a mountain peak and palm trees and fishing boats in a tropical harbor; the general coloration was green and blue (or, according to Scott with its painterly precision, viridian and aquamarine), and there was a title beneath: *Los Pescadores*. Keen-eyed, I had no trouble picking out the fishermen themselves, who were Negroes and wore white turbans and were busy at work tending their nets against a backdrop of aquamarine harbor and viridian mountains, behind which the sun appeared to be setting. There were other stamps in my collection that I greatly admired—a huge Greek airmail in gorgeous pastel facets, rather like stained glass; a gaudy number from Guatemala featuring a quetzal bird with streaming tail feathers; a glossy octagonal from Hejaz festooned with Arabic script; the Nyasaland triangle, shaped to accommodate spindly-legged giraffes—but none so arrested my imagination or so whetted my longing for faraway places as the one from that archipelago whose name itself was an incantation: *Elobey, Annobón, and Corisco.*

Back on Saipan I found myself an unwilling visitor to one of those faraway places of my stamp collection and yearned for nothing better than to be stretched out on the floor of the living room, merely dreaming of one of those places rather than being actually in one. In the tent, half-drowsing in the wicked heat, I would convert my identity into that of a small boy again, re-creating in memory ever younger incarnations of myself. In the stamp collection sequence, for example, it would be Sunday afternoon: sprawled on the crimson rug I would lick little cellophane hinges while my mother, her steel-braced leg propped on a stool beneath an afghan, read the sepia-tinted rotogravure section of the *New York Times,* and my father, seated at the antique walnut secretary, penned one of his innumerable letters regarding the Whitehurst family genealogy. Warm, too warm (for in the winter my mother was always cold), the room contained the lingering smell of the roast chicken we had eaten for Sunday dinner, and the whole sunny space, cocoon-like, was wrapped in layers and layers of sound: the New York Philharmonic from the table-top Zenith radio. Forest horns and kettledrums. Swollen ecstasy. Johannes Brahms. Sunday's murmurous purple melancholy.

Another scene from a younger time: my father alongside me as we lay at the edge of the bank above the muddy James. He was teaching me to shoot. The .22 bullets were greasy to the fingertips, the odor of burnt powder both sweet and pungent as the casings flew from the chamber. Squ*eeze* slowly, he would murmur, and my heart would skip a beat when I saw the green whiskey bottle turn to flying shards in the sand. Younger, much younger, I felt the ceramic bowl chill against my legs while he taught me accuracy in peeing. *Stand close, son* were his words; *hit the hole.* I couldn't locate any memories of my father earlier than this, nor of the protectiveness and safety he embodied for his son lost in the Pacific distances. Anything earlier than this would have meant oblivion, prememory, only my father's seed and my mother's womb. And that womb, likewise protective and safe, was from time to time another place I longed for in the persistent ache of my dread.

For in truth the embryonic fear I'd felt on the ship had swollen hugely. I was scared nearly to death. While previously Okinawa had been an exciting place to dream about, an island where I would exploit my potential for bravery, now the idea of going back there nearly sickened me. Thus I found myself in a conflict I had never anticipated: afraid of going into battle, yet even more afraid of betraying my fear, which would be an ugly prelude to the most harrowing fear of all—that when forced to the test in combat I would demonstrate my absolute terror, fall apart, and fail my fellow marines. These intricately intertwined fears began to torment me without letup. And though I continued my jaunty masquerade, more often than not dread won out. And when that happened I would seek my tent, if I had the chance, and lie on my cot gazing upward at the stitch and weave of the canvas, and try to exorcise the dread, whispering: *Elobey, Annobón, and Corisco.*

PUBLISHER'S NOTE

The Suicide Run consists of five narratives by William Styron, one previously unpublished and four never before collected. All five are drawn from Styron's experiences in the U.S. Marine Corps. Together they present a complex picture of military life—its hardships, deprivations, and stupidities; its esprit, camaraderie, and seductive allure.

"Blankenship," written during the summer of 1953, was first published in the journal *Papers on Language and Literature* in a special issue (Autumn 1987) devoted to Styron's work. "Marriott, the Marine" and "The Suicide Run" were composed in the early 1970s as parts of "The Way of the Warrior," a novel that Styron put aside to write *Sophie's Choice* (1979). "Marriott" was first published in the September 1971 issue of *Esquire*; "The Suicide Run" appeared initially in the *American Poetry Review* for May/June 1974. "My Father's House" is the opening section of an unfinished novel, begun in 1985, that Styron intended to base on his experiences during the spring and summer of 1946, just after he had been discharged from the Marine Corps. The middle portion of "My Father's House" appeared in *The New Yorker,* under the title "Rat Beach," in the double fiction issue for July 6/13, 2009. The vignette "Elobey, Annobón, and Corisco," previously unpublished, was composed in 1995.

The text of "Blankenship" is based on the surviving typescript in the William Styron Papers, Manuscripts Division, Library of Congress. The text of "Marriott, the Marine" is taken from its appearance in *Esquire,* with corrections from the manuscript in the Styron collection at the W. R. Perkins Library, Duke University. The setting-copy typescript of "The Suicide Run"—preserved in the archives of the *American Poetry Review,* Annenberg Rare Book and Manuscript Library, University of Pennsylvania—is the source for the text published in this volume. Texts for "My Father's House" and "Elobey, Annobón, and Corisco" have been established from extant manuscripts and typescripts in the Styron papers at Duke.

ABOUT THE TYPE

This book was set in Fairfield, the first typeface from the hand of the distinguished American artist and engraver Rudolph Ruzicka (1883–1978). Ruzicka was born in Bohemia and came to America in 1894. He set up his own shop, devoted to wood engraving and printing, in New York in 1913 after a varied career working as a wood engraver, in photoengraving and banknote printing plants, and as an art director and freelance artist. He designed and illustrated many books, and was the creator of a considerable list of individual prints—wood engravings, line engravings on copper, and aquatints.